I'm Boo . . . That's Who!

by Diana Gregory

illustrations by Susan Spellman Mohn

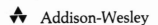 Addison-Wesley

Text copyright © 1979 by Diana Gregory
Illustrations copyright © 1979 by Susan Spellman Mohn
All Rights Reserved
Addison-Wesley Publishing Company, Inc.
Reading, Massachusetts 01867
Printed in the United States of America
ABCDEFGHIJK-DO-79

Library of Congress Cataloging in Publication Data

Gregory, Diana.
  I'm Boo . . . that's who!

  SUMMARY: After moving from Los Angeles to a small
town in the Virginia horse country, 13-year-old Boo comes
to the reluctant conclusion that the only way to make
friends is to join the local stable and learn to ride.
  [1. Horsemanship—Fiction. 2. Friendship—Fiction.
3. Moving, Household—Fiction] I. Mohn, Susan Spellman.
II. Title.
PZ7.G8618Im   [Fic]   79-15626
ISBN 0-201-02628-7

For Lisa . . .
and her Big Blue

My name is Boo Hedley.

It's been Boo for nearly eleven years now, ever since I was about two years old. I guess just about everyone has forgotten that the name I was born with is Lisa.

I got the name Boo because, at the time, the only intelligent thing I'd learned how to say was "boo-boo." Probably everybody referred to me as the "boo-boo" kid and the name stuck. Mom sometimes says she doesn't think I've improved all that much on my intelligence since then.

Take how I got this stupid cast on my leg. But, then, I don't say breaking my leg was my fault. No! Not on your life. The fault was Jonathan's. If it wasn't for him and that stupid snake of his I wouldn't be here. I would be out swimming at Chris Green Lake with everyone else.

But there I go, shooting off in all directions and not telling you the story. Miss Martha Pritchard Godalming, my English teacher from last year, told me time and time again that my writing is totally disorganized and that if I am ever to get an acceptable grade in a composition class I must learn to put things in order and start with a written outline. But I hate writing outlines. So I hope that you will bear with me until I get things started and the people involved all in order. Because once I do I become fairly consistent and the story (even one as horrifying as this) rolls right along to the conclusion.

I'll start at the beginning—then maybe you'll have an idea as to what everything is all about and agree with me on whose fault it is.

Listen! I know you should start at the beginning. Of course that's where you should start. But sometimes it is kind of difficult to decide just where the beginning of something is, especially when it's from real life and not just make-believe.

I think this particular beginning happened about three months ago, while I was still living in California.

It was on a Saturday afternoon and not exactly one of those winner days that Californians are always bragging about. We were in the midst of a smog alert and because of that I was staying inside and watching an old 1930s detective movie on TV. (I love old 1930s detective movies and probably would have been watching this particular one anyway as it was a really terrific Thin Man one. But the smog alert gave me an excuse so I didn't have to explain myself to anyone.)

Then, just as Nick Charles was hustling this anthropoidal-looking gangster into making the mistake of a lifetime, Mom came home from shopping and made her announcement—without even waiting for the commercial break, so I knew it must be pretty important.

"Boo," she said, "I've had it with this smog. Start packing. We're moving to Virginia."

Well, the smog really was bad that day. I've already told you that. Anyone with half a brain would pack up and move about as far away as you could possibly get from the stuff. And Virginia was certainly that, being on the exact opposite side of the country from California. But most people either can't or won't just up and leave like that. At least your everyday average family doesn't. However, it has been brought to my attention more than once that we are not exactly your average American family (if there is such a thing). You know, the kind they show a lot in Walt Disney movies.

To start with we are a one-adult family. I know, I know. That's pretty average nowadays. But not when the one adult, though she is a pretty super Mom most times, needs a keeper to look after her the rest of the time.

Mom is a freelance artist. That means she does her artwork for a lot of different people—not just one —so she is really her own boss. But because she is an artist she gets kind of flighty and temperamental every once in a while. We don't live in an attic, or anything like that, and she doesn't paint stuff that you can't tell what it is. She does illustrations for books, like of knights slaying dragons and that sort of thing.

She's good enough at it so we don't have to worry about where our next jar of peanut butter is coming from and my allowance is paid fairly regularly. Our family vacations are spent driving to someplace like Yellowstone Park instead of flying off to Hawaii, like I wish we would. But at least we do have vacations. Also I don't have to nag too much when I want a new pair of jeans or the latest Al Stewart tape, but I do have to try and make one pair of shoes last through a school year. (Can anybody do that? I get to about April 27 and that's it.)

That part's pretty average. It's just Mom's emotional level that puts us out of the average class. Though it's only when she's really depressed. When that happens she doesn't cry or go out and buy something new or throw dishes or any of those things, which are over and done with so that you can forget about them after a day or so and go on with everyday matters. No! When she is really depressed we move. And I don't mean to just another house.

She gets this way about once a year. So, since it had been eleven months since our last move, I could figure it was about time for the next one. The fact that the day was overly gucky with everyone's thoughtless pollution was just an excuse to move. Sort of like it was my excuse for lying around and watching an old 1930s flick.

Anyway, I wasn't too surprised at the announcement Mom made. I didn't get all excited and jump up and start asking questions like you probably would if your mom came home and said that to you. Instead I said, "Right after this movie, OK, Mom?" Then I went into a depression of my own and forgot all about the neat things the Thin Man was doing to the gangster who resembled an ape.

I stuffed the rest of my cheese and peanut butter sandwich into my mouth and started picking at my thumbnail while thinking glum thoughts about having to move again. I hate it! And I hate hating it because it makes me hate Mom for a while. Not really, but almost—at least until we are all moved and into another place again.

I think if I were given just one real wish in this world it would be that we would finally settle down in one spot and stay there. I don't think it would matter where, just so I could make friends that I knew I could keep and go through school with and not just have an overstuffed address book that is filled with names of kids who I've promised to write to forever and then do write to for a while and then less and less and then not at all.

Maybe it'll happen someday. But I'm not going to count on it.

Now that I think about it, it is probably this one weirdness (is that a word?) of Mom's that has made Jonathan the creep that he is. You remember, I just told you about him. He's my brother and the other human (if you can call anyone like Jonathan human) member of our family group.

He is absolutely unreal. Most kids at the age of nine would be happy to put in their quota of TV watching, if not more, and do it while munching some good, wholesome, junk food. Not Jonathan. At the age of three, or thereabout, he decided he wanted to become a biophysicist (whatever that is). I haven't seen his face, from the eyebrows south, since then due to the constant presence of a book heavy enough to make him a hunchback for life. As for foodstuffs, he is a vegetarian freak. He consumes only goat's milk, organic fruits and vegetables, and mung bean sprouts, which he grows by the acre in an old aquarium in his room.

Also in that aquarium lives Jonathan's constant companion and bosom friend—Wentworth. Just so you'll understand why I bother to mention Wentworth at all (because most times it is best not to mention snakes as not too many people are thrilled with the subject), it is because he plays such an important part in the story, being the hero to some and the villain to others.

But I must give Wentworth his due. He is almost lovable (I said *almost*) because he is so unsnakelike. Most snakes are content to eat once or twice a month and thereby keep their slim, snakelike figure. Not Wentworth. Wentworth is a munchmouth. And because of that he has lost any slitherlike qualities he might have otherwise possessed. Instead, he resembles a rather long and squishy Polish sausage. He pretty much stays put wherever Jonathan puts him, his main activities being eating and napping. This makes me, though not totally happy, at least content in that I know I am not going to be surprised by finding Wentworth in various places that I would prefer not to find him in.

I guess the blame for Wentworth's condition could be placed at Mom's feet. Mom can't stand cruelty to animals in any form. A lot of snakes in captivity have to be fed live chicks and mice in order to keep them happy and thriving. But Mom wasn't having any of that nonsense. So Wentworth got fed hamburger meat with a few chicken feathers stuck in it to try and fool him into thinking it was a baby chick. He seemed to like it. In fact, pretty soon we noticed that he wouldn't touch the part with the feathers in it, and after a while things evolved down to where Wentworth's diet now consists of a McDonald's cheeseburger—hold the pickle and add plenty of catsup —every other day. This galls Jonathan, being as how he is a vegetarian, and if he had it his way Wentworth would be munching on goat cheese. Nevertheless, Wentworth is happy and I guess that is what counts.

I was still sitting there in front of the TV, though I had switched to working on the other thumbnail, when Mom, who had been impatiently waiting on the sidelines, came over and snapped off the set and stood there with an expectant look of mixed excitement and hope that I would be as delighted by the idea as she obviously was. But this time I wasn't playing the game no matter how much I knew she wanted me to. I knew it was hopeless to even try to reason with her, but I did anyway.

"Look, Mom," I said, "I know the smog is a real killer today and it probably will be tomorrow. But, honest, that's no reason to move. And it would mean that we'd have to go through all the closets and clean out everything just when we've finally found places for everything, and—"

"Oh, poo, Boo," Mom broke in. "That's no reason to either move or stay. What's important is getting away from this unhealthy smog. And if we can move to a place where the air is clean and there is a little culture and tradition as well, I say it is a splendid idea."

"But—"

"And I don't want to argue about it because I already have a house lined up and I called the movers while you were watching the rest of your movie. They're coming on Friday morning."

Wow! I thought. Mom's moving faster than usual. What cooks? Aloud I said, "You've got a house lined up! How did you do that? What did you do—make a detour through Virginia on your way to the A & P?"

"Don't get smart, Boo," Mom warned, with just a bit more irritation showing than usual when I make a crack like that. "No. It just so happens that a friend of one of the people I work for is leaving for Europe for a year and is looking for someone to stay in his house and take care of it while he is gone. Naturally I thought it was a perfect opportunity for you and Jonathan to get to see that part of the country."

Here I groaned, having seen far more of the country already than I want to. I got another stern look for my effort.

"There's Washington, D.C., not too far away and several historic towns such as Williamsburg and Jamestown. Not only that," and here she absolutely beamed as if she were about to tell me something really great like Dustin Hoffman was to be our new neighbor, "the house is in the middle of the famous Virginia horse country. You can take riding lessons, be in horse shows, and just have a grand time." She stooped over and gave me a peck on the forehead. "Now, I've got a million things to do if we're to leave by Friday."

Mom zoomed out, her batteries charged to the max and ready to take care of those million things all at once. Me, I sat there staring at the blank TV screen wishing it was a couple of hours earlier when I was happy and content and looking forward to watching the Thin Man do his thing. But it wasn't. What I was looking forward to, and not at all contentedly, was sorting out my junk and getting to the bottom of my closet to find out what was down there that was worth taking and packing all my stuffed animals into boxes and adding more names to my address book and . . .

. . . learning how to ride a horse. Really terrific! I don't even like horses.

2

My mom is one of those compulsive travelers who just has to get going at the crack of dawn or she feels the entire day has been a waste. Consequently, after the movers have gone, she packs the station wagon with everything else and we settle down to spend the night sleeping on folded blankets on the floor. This results in no one being able to really sleep. Then some time during the night, usually about 3:30, we find ourselves being herded, half asleep, into the station wagon and on our way.

This time was no exception. By now, though, I am so used to it that I do it almost automatically and I barely left dreamland. So it wasn't until about three hours later, when the sun was starting to come up and shine through the windshield into my face, that I started to come awake.

You know how it is when you are half asleep. You kind of have difficulty orienting yourself and tend to think you are where you are not. I thought, at first, that I was still back in Los Angeles in my white French provincial   pink-and-white-gingham-canopied   bed with the rickrack on the edges that is coming unsewn. I reached over to cuddle Big Blue and try and go back to sleep until it was time to get up.

Big Blue is a very special person who has lived with me since before I can remember and always sleeps with me instead of on the window seat with my other stuffed animals.

I reached out my hand to where he usually sleeps on the pillow next to mine. But he wasn't there, and neither was the pillow. Instead there was one of those flimsy cardboard boxes you get from a takeout place. This particular one contained a half-eaten jelly donut and an almost empty cup of cold coffee. Into which I put my hand. Let me say, right here and now, that this sort of thing is guaranteed to bring a person to absolutely complete and total wakefulness (is wakefulness a word?) in a hurry.

Anyway, this particular wakefulness brought with it an instant panic, the likes of which is hard to put into words. For I suddenly realized that the reason Big Blue was not there beside me was that he was tucked away inside the window seat in my room back at our old house, where I had put him out of harm's way so he wouldn't be trampled on during the disaster scene that usually accompanies one of our moves. So, with-

out a minute's hesitation I sat up and screamed
—STOP THE CAR!

There is nothing wrong with Mom's reflexes and what she did then was STOP THE CAR—right in the middle of a four-lane highway. Fortunately we happened to be the only ones occupying that particular stretch of roadway so there weren't any major collisions. But there was almost an accident right there inside the car when Mom realized I wasn't telling her to stop because some animal was about to run out in front of us, or because Jonathan was about to fall out of a rear door (worse luck)—but because Big Blue was missing.

To say she was miffed is to put it mildly. Since we hadn't really been hitting it off too well since she'd made the decision to pack us off to the other side of the country, this kind of put the topper on it. She pulled over to the side of the road and sat there fuming and drinking the rest of the cold coffee (that I had put my hand into, but I didn't tell her that).

For a while I was pretty worried. I was ready to tell Mom I would walk back and get Big Blue if I had to. But she's actually a pretty understanding parent even when she is mad. She didn't say a word. She started the car and turned around and headed back where we had just come from. She didn't say a word for the three hours that it took us to get back to our old house. And she didn't say a word but just sat there in the car looking straight ahead after she gave me the house key. But she had come back. I went into the house to rescue Big Blue.

I didn't let on to Big Blue that he had almost been left behind. I got him out of the window seat and hugged him and told him how much I loved him. Then I sat down on the window seat and explained to him that we were moving again but it wasn't such a big deal just as long as we were together and maybe the place we were going to might be even nicer than the one we were leaving.

I didn't really believe all that and I really do know that Big Blue is a stuffed animal and not a real person. But I think I had to say those things out loud or bust because I had been silent about my feelings for too many days, what with thinking bad thoughts about the trip and the move. Now maybe I could straighten things out in my own mind. Also, because Mom had been so good (well, she had) about coming back all that way to get Big Blue, I supposed that if this move would make her happy then I wanted it to be OK.

I took a last look around my old room, which was now empty of furniture, and it didn't seem to be home any more anyway. I mustered up the best smile I could and went back out and got in the car. I leaned over and kissed Mom on the cheek and said, "Thanks." She stopped looking straight ahead and smiled back, then hugged me—just the way I had hugged Big Blue. She got the car going and said, "OK, let's get this show on the road." And we did.

About an hour later, after Jonathan had finally woken up, she asked us if we were hungry. We all agreed we were so we pulled into a McDonald's and had breakfast. For the first time in five days I realized I really was hungry. I had pancakes and sausage and milk, and Mom had some hot coffee and an English muffin. Because he had fruit and cheese in a cooler in the car, Jonathan just drank three cartons of milk. Then, even though they hadn't started making hamburgers yet, Mom got them to make a cheeseburger for Wentworth. And we were on our way again.

It's a funny thing about driving across the country. No matter how often you drive around in it you never seem to get over the idea that the states should look like they do in the atlas and that you should be able to tell when you go from one to another by the colors. You know, like the countries in Oz with Arizona being one color and Texas being another and so on. But they aren't. Instead there are a lot of different sections that have nothing to do with state borders, and those change so gradually that you don't realize you are going from one to another until you're through them and on the other side.

After we left southern California, which is really a lot of little towns stuck so close together that it seems the entire state is just one big city, we started driving across a big desert. In fact the desert went on and on and on for about three days, or four. I lost track I think because all the motels and the coffee shops look pretty much alike and you just travel along with the rest of the cars headed in the same direction.

After a while you start to recognize some of the ones that are traveling in the same direction as you.

And if there are kids in the cars you wave at each other every time you meet.

It was somewhere in Texas that we latched on to a car with a boy and a girl about my age. We had been following this dark green station wagon for about an hour and the girl had waved a couple of times at me and I had waved back. Then she finally poked the boy, who had been reading a book, and he looked up and waved too. Then I saw him scrounging around in a cardboard carton for something and pretty soon he was holding up a sign that said *HI!*

Then I scarfed around and found a piece of paper and wrote back *HI—I'M BOO—WHO ARE YOU?* and held it up against the windshield on my side of the car.

(Jonathan wasn't having any of this stuff. His nose was deep in some book from the library that he hadn't returned and that Mom was going to have to mail back as soon as we got to Virginia.)

After about a mile the kids in the other car put up another sign. *WE'RE SANDY AND TERRY.* Then they turned it over and it read *YOU'RE WHO?* (I told you people sometimes act strange about my name.)

So I turned my sign over and printed *I'M BOO THAT'S WHO* and showed that.

Then you could see them looking at each other and cracking up over that and the next sign that came up read *RIGHT!* And you could tell we were friends.

But then their car slowed down and they pulled into a coffee shop. I wanted to stay with them and thought about asking Mom to stop so we could get a Coke or something. But we had eaten just a little before that so I knew it would be a dumb thing to ask. I was sorry we were going on without them, but I had a feeling we would be seeing each other again. So later when we did stop I got Mom to let me go into a drugstore that was nearby and get a large pad of paper and a marking pen so I'd be prepared next time we did meet, which we did later on that afternoon. Our two cars stayed pretty much together for the rest of the day and from their signs I learned that they were moving, too, and that they were on their way to Kentucky, which is right next to Virginia.

That night we got our respective parents to stop so we could all have dinner together. Then, because we were already stopped at one of those restaurants that has a motel as well, we all ended up spending the night there. So I really got a good chance to talk to them and I found out that their family moved a lot too because their dad works for a company that transfers him around the country almost as often as we move. They weren't too keen about it either, but their dad couldn't help it. Anyway it was nice to talk to someone else who was going through the same thing.

We made up some games we could play using the signs. Actually they were the usual car games you play whenever you are driving any distance at all. You know, each of you sees who can get the most license plates from different states or find letters in billboards and road signs until you've completed the alphabet. Only instead of competing with someone in your own car we were teams—the blue station wagon versus the dark green one. Even Jonathan got intrigued because it had something to do with mathematical odds. And that was the way we spent the next two days, until they had to turn off the main highway.

Before they did, though, both cars stopped at a rest stop and we shared a sort of ceremonial watermelon between families and exchanged addresses so I had one more to put into my address book. But this one was different. We were fellow travelers with a lot in common. And if we kept moving about we would no doubt run into one another again sometime. The world is small that way and those things do happen.

The rest of the trip didn't seem so long after that. As I said, sometimes you aren't aware of the change in scenery until after it has happened. That was the case here. I started paying attention. The world was no longer wall-to-wall desert and dirt. Now it was trees, lots of them, and lakes, lots of them, and once in a while you could spot a deer in among the trees. I started to get excited. It was really pretty. A lot greener than California, or any place else we had lived.

Then, as we drove along, I noticed that the towns were definite towns and there was country in between so they weren't all run together. I started making up stories to myself as to what it would be like living in the particular town we were passing at the time. I began to wonder what the town we were headed for would be like. I tried to picture the school and where the kids would hang out and what those kids were like. And the more I thought about it and made up situations the more excited I got, though I wasn't showing any of this reaction to Mom. Then from excited I got nervous and even a little frightened. What if the kids in our new town didn't like me or thought I was strange because I didn't come from their part of the country? I sank down into myself and stopped noticing what was happening outside the car windows.

It was late in the afternoon and I figured we would be stopping for the night pretty soon. Sure enough, at the next town Mom started slowing down and looking for an off-ramp. There was a good motel just ahead and I hoped there would be a pool because I was hot and tired and could sure use a swim. But suddenly we were past the motel and driving down the main street.

"Hey Mom," I said, "What gives? There wasn't a *No Vacancy* sign. Why didn't we stop there?" Then I noticed that Mom had that kind of triumphant smile she gets when we've finally reached where we're going. I sat up straight and said "hey" again, but this time it was "HEY!"

"That's right, Boo. This is it. Now if you'll help me by looking for a street called Emmet, I think we can find the house before it gets dark."

Well, I started looking. But it wasn't for the street sign and we had already gone about a hundred feet past it when Jonathan piped up and said something downgrading about my mentality and told Mom that we had passed it years back.

"That's OK," Mom said, not sounding a bit upset. So I knew she was excited, too. "Boo's probably just tired." She made a U-turn at the next corner and went back to Emmet. We turned left and followed Emmet for about six blocks to a street called Dogwood Place, and that's where we turned next. Mom slowed the car down to a crawl and we all started looking for house numbers.

"Look for 167," she said. "It's supposed to be a two-story yellow house with a lot of gingerbread and a white front porch."

Well, most of the houses were two-storied ones and most of them had wide front porches, but there was only one yellow one and that was halfway down the next block. I shouted that I'd seen it and pointed. I realized I was a little scared. I had that squiggly feeling you get in the pit of your stomach when you're hoping for the best and fearing the worst. I wanted it to turn out to be a nice house so badly. I closed my eyes and when the car stopped I waited and said a little prayer before I opened my eyes, fast.

And it was!

Mom was already on the front walk and telling me to hurry up and didn't I want to see what it looked like inside.

It was a great house!

I got out of the car and joined Mom on the front walk and was looking up at it and taking it all in—the little cupola on top with the wrought-iron weather vane and the scalloped shingles on the roof and the fantastic porch with all that gingerbread making it look like a giant frosted Christmas cookie.

Mom was ahead of me again, standing at the front door and searching in her purse for the key. We smiled at each other and I went on up to where she was. But just as I got there I heard one of the loudest screams I have ever head in my entire life. We both looked to see where it was coming from and there on the porch next door was a girl with long blond hair. She was standing and screaming and pointing at the walk I had just come up.

I knew it! I knew it before I even looked. But I looked anyway. I saw what I thought I would see —Jonathan standing there with Wentworth draped around his neck.

And that is how I met Tamara!

3

There's only one little thing that bothers me about Tamara and that is that she is prettier than I am. That's not just my opinion. Tamara told me that herself.

We'd met briefly last night after she'd stopped screaming. Mom, being the diplomat that she can be sometimes, had told Jonathan to take Wentworth back to the car and lock him up in his cage. She'd said that overly loud so that the girl next door would know that Wentworth wasn't going to go anywhere. Then she looked at me and twitched her head in my direction, so that I knew I was going to be involved as well, and together we walked across the connecting lawn to where the girl was still standing, up on her front porch, and looking as though she didn't want to have anything to do with anyone who had anything to do with Wentworth. But Mom soon soothed that over by telling her that Wentworth was perfectly harmless and was always locked up tight so she needn't worry. Which is really a white lie because Wentworth is never locked up. It is just that he rarely moves at all and if he were a stone he would probably have gathered a ton of moss by now.

So then Mom introduced herself and, of course, me and said we were moving in next door. Tamara put on a bright smile and said how glad she was. I put on a bright smile and said how thrilled I was. Of course, all the while I was putting on my bright smile and saying that, I was wondering what she was really thinking. What I was thinking was that I very much wanted a large hole to open up in front of me so that I could jump into it and pull the top over me.

Then Mom did the most incredible thing—but I should have known she would. She said something, most of which I didn't catch except that it ended in her having to do a million things (why is it always a million?) and wouldn't I like to stay out here for awhile and get better acquainted with Tamara.

No, Mom, no, I screamed silently. The smile on my face was beginning to get a little tight and then I realized that I was still smiling and that Tamara must think I was either a mummified idiot or practicing to be a jack-o-lantern for next Halloween. So I let it collapse and out loud said "Sure."

Then Tamara picked up the cue and, with that sort of bouncy attitude that immediately tells you that this girl is popular, went all hostessy and asked me if I'd like some iced tea and then offered some to Mom as well.

Naturally Mom declined and made her exit, leaving me standing there wondering if I looked as rumpled and ugly as I thought I did. After all, when you've just ridden about five hundred miles in a hot car with your head hanging halfway out of the window in order to keep cool, you don't exactly look like Miss America. I put a hand casually up to my hair and immediately knew the answer. But I was stuck. I followed Tamara in through her house to the kitchen and stood there feeling awkward while she got out glasses and ice and a pitcher of tea from the refrigerator.

When she'd poured the tea she handed me a glass and suggested that we go back out to the front porch where it was cooler and sit on the swing.

She sat on the swing. I said something stupid like the swing reminded me too much of the car that I'd just been in for three thousand miles and sat on the steps instead. Actually I didn't want to sit too close to her. First, it makes me nervous to sit close to someone I've just met, and second, I didn't want her to make too close a comparison between us. I mean she looked like she came out of one of those TV commercials that shows someone just out of the shower and looking all beautiful and ready for a date. Her long blonde hair was straight and shiny. She swung it around a lot, and it went awfully well with a really fabulous tan. I

wondered how she had gotten that so early in the summer. After all, school had ended only a week or so ago, and even after I have spent the entire summer slathered in tanning oil I never look like that. And a lot of that tan was on these incredibly long slim legs that she had stretched out in front of her while she wiggled ten perfectly painted pink toenails.

Now I'm not bad looking, you understand. But it is this type of person that truly deflates my ego. I am only a little over five feet tall and aware of every inch I lack. Though I spent a year and a half taking gymnastics and hanging on bars in hopes that I would stretch, I know that it is to be my fate to remain short for the rest of my life. As for my hair, I am cursed with a head full of fuzzy brown curls. I tried growing it out once and did everything from ironing it to spending a fortune for a body perm in order to make it straight. But it didn't work and I ended up cutting it off again.

We'd been quiet and sitting there sipping on our tea while I was doing all this comparison thinking, and then I realized that she had been doing the same thing because she came out and said it, just like that. She put her head on one side, looked at me, took a sip of her tea, and said, "I like your hair. It suits you. You're the cute type. I'm the pretty type. That's good. Because that way we'll never have to feel we're competing with each other when it comes to boys." Then she smiled in that bouncy way that was somehow friendly as well. She giggled and put her hand, the one that wasn't holding the iced tea, on top of her head and said, "Oh, my gosh! Can you believe I said that?"

Then I felt better and laughed and admitted that I'd been doing some comparison thinking myself and I'd come up with about the same thing. I took another sip of my tea and she did too, and then we made the mistake of looking at each other because she crossed her eyes and then we both tried to swallow our tea before we burst out laughing but we didn't make it and tea went all over the front porch.

I relaxed and all of a sudden there were about a million (there's that million again, but this time I said it) things I wanted to ask her. About the schools and places to go and what everybody did during the summer and boys.

As to boys I, myself, haven't really had that much to do with them up until now. Mom laid down the rule early that there was to be absolutely no dating until I am fourteen, and then no car dates until I'm sixteen. But I figure I might as well start researching the subject now. However, I didn't want Tamara to know my status. What if she already dated and was way ahead of me and might think I was dumb or that I had a fogie for a parent? Though I think Mom is right in that I haven't really felt all that ready for boys up until now and it's kind of nice to have rules laid down by a parent as an excuse you can use so that you can say you can't when you don't really want to but don't want the person who's asking you to do something to know you don't want to. Do you understand what I mean?

So I didn't say anything about boys right away. Instead I asked her how she got her tan.

"Oh, I tan easily. But all the kids start going out to Chris Green Lake every weekend from Easter vacation on, and by now mostly everyone has one. That's because we spend most of the summer riding and don't have all the time to spend getting one then."

Blast, I thought. That word sounded familiar. "Riding, did you say. You mean on horses?"

"Of course on horses, you ninny. What else, water buffaloes? I'm sorry. I shouldn't have said that. Don't you ride? But then I guess you wouldn't, coming from Los Angeles."

Mom had mentioned that we had come from Los Angeles when she was making introductions. And yes, of course we have horses in Los Angeles, but I certainly hadn't wanted to ride them.

"Well," I said, "we spent a lot of time riding bikes and playing tennis and things like that. But I'd really love to learn how to ride (oh, super lie) and Mom's already promised to let me have lessons (that's true) and I can hardly wait to start (double super lie)."

"That's terrific!" (Wouldn't you know that's what she'd say!) "Listen! Why don't you go out with me to the stable tomorrow morning. That is if you're not too tired or have a lot of unpacking to do or anything like that. If you can't, maybe sometime next week."

I know how it is when you are new any place. (I ought to.) When someone makes an offer like that you don't turn it down. If I said no now, it might make me sound like a dud and she'd think twice about making another offer, or she might get busy and forget to ask again. So if I didn't play the game right and go when asked, I just jolly well might be spending the entire summer sitting on my own front porch swing, by myself, waiting for school to open. So I said the only thing I could say.

"Terrific! I'd love to."

"Great! That way you can meet everyone and get started on your lessons right away. The kids are really super and I know they'll love meeting you. New blood and all that sort of thing. We haven't had anyone new move in for ages. We all sort of grew up together and we are so used to each other that we take everyone for granted."

Oh, boy! That meant I would probably have to work doubly hard in order to be accepted into the group. When a bunch of kids is that tightly put together it is almost impossible to break in. Well, I was going to give it the old Hedley try.

It had gotten nearly dark. Funny, I hadn't noticed. I guess we'd been talking longer than I thought we had. Mom came out from our house next door and yelled that she was sorry but it was time to leave. Then she went out to the car and got in, and I knew that meant now. I stood up and handed Tamara my glass. She had stood up when Mom called and had come over to the steps next to me.

"Don't forget about tomorrow. I leave for the stable about ten. If you don't make it though, don't worry. But I hope you can. And I'm really glad you're going to live next door."

"I am too . . . glad that I'm going to be living next door. And I will definitely see you tomorrow at ten. 'Nite." I ran down the steps to join Mom in the car. And I found I really was glad.

Mom said that the movers wouldn't be there until the day after the next so we'd be staying at the motel we'd passed earlier, but that she'd be more than glad to drive me back out in the morning so I could go with Tamara. I could hardly wait.

*   *   *

But that was last night. Now it was morning and I was standing in the motel room looking into the dirty mess that was my suitcase and beginning to panic because I couldn't find anything to wear. I almost wished I hadn't been so positive when I said I'd be there. As I sat down on the edge of the bed holding a T-shirt with a dried blob of mustard on it, I wished that Tamara wasn't so pretty!

4

Why didn't you wash something out last night for heaven's sake?"

That was Mom's answer to my cry of pain over having nothing to wear. I would have said something in my defense, but I knew she was right. I should have, but you know how it is when you're really beat and all you can think of is how fast you can fall into bed. You rationalize to yourself that you'll get up early, rinse something out, squeeze it out in a towel, and then dry it with the hair blower. But when morning does come you roll over and stuff your head under the pillow for two more minutes. When you finally do get up it's too late and you're sitting there wondering what on earth to put on. Just as I was doing now. So instead what I did was groan and fall back on the bed and say, "I won't go."

"Nonsense," was Mom's reply. "You probably have something clean down under that mess and you haven't really tried looking for it. Here, let me see." And right away she was burrowing into my things, scattering the dirty ones right and left like some worrisome hedgehog.

"I thought so." This as she triumphantly held up a purple-and-white-striped T-shirt that somehow I had missed. "Now put this on, brush your hair, and let's get going. It's almost ten o'clock. You told that girl you'd be there and you will be."

I yanked the shirt out of Mom's hand, grumbled something, and went into the bathroom to finish getting ready. Secretly I really do appreciate the way Mom always takes things in hand just as I am about to give up; she makes me get back on my feet. It is nice to know that's the way she works. But I'm sure not going to ever let on I feel that way. I'm afraid if I do she'll stop.

Mom drove a little faster than she usually does and we got to where our new house was slightly after 10:15. Tamara was getting into the passenger side of a yellow Datsun when Mom pulled up to the curb and gave a little honk to let her know we were there. She looked up and waved. The lady driving looked over and waved too. She was obviously Tamara's mother. She looked a lot like Tamara, only older, and instead of having long straight hair she had one of those set styles that looks like it should come off at night and sit on the dresser and then be put on again in the morning. As soon as I'd gotten out of the car Mom waved again and then drove off. It was that kind of thing where you don't get out of your car and go and talk to the person because you know this is not the time, but you want to show you are friendly all the same. Mom was cool that way and I liked her for that.

Tamara stood next to the Datsun's door and waited until I had slid into the middle of the front seat. Then she got in next to me so that I was sitting pushed together between her and her mother. She was still her bouncy self this morning. And when she introduced me to her mother I found out right away where all this bounciness came from, because her Mom was bouncy in her own way.

As I said before, I don't really like getting too close to people I am meeting for the first time, and being stuck between these two bouncy people, like a blob of tuna fish salad between two pieces of white toast, was certainly what you might call close. But it's funny, somehow I didn't mind this time. For some strange reason I suddenly felt as though I had known these two people for a long time and that we had been neighbors for years and I belonged here on my way to wherever we were going. Perhaps it was a trick of my imagination brought on by the long trip from California and because I was so far away from my last home. I felt like some time traveler who had finally ended up back where he belonged, but because where he belonged was still in the future he didn't know it yet.

All those thoughts went through my head in the space it took for Tamara's mother to back out of the driveway, change gears, and head off down the street toward where the edge of town should be. Then I was back to myself, and I was kind of sorry about that.

"Tamara says you don't ride, Boo, but that you're planning on taking lessons," Tamara's mother said in that tone mothers of popular girls always seem to have.

"Yes, Mrs. Hunter," I replied in a tone I hoped she'd approve of. "I've been thinking about it ever since my mother told me we were moving to Virginia and that mostly everyone here rides."

Mrs. Hunter laughed and said, "Not everyone, Boo. Frankly, I'd rather sit and watch."

Idly I wondered what would happen to my social life if I admitted I would rather sit and watch, too. Probably I would be drummed right out of the state of Virginia.

"Boo's right," Tamara jumped in. "Just about everybody does ride, and she's dying to learn. Aren't you, Boo?" She turned her bright smile on at me.

"Oh, yes!" (What else could I say?)

"Well, Jim Sikes is about the best riding instructor in Virginia," Mrs. Hunter went on. "You couldn't be in better hands. And it's nice that you're starting at the beginning of summer. That way you can probably be in the horse show that we have at the end of summer."

"Oh, good thinking, Mom." Tamara said. "I didn't even consider that. And we really need someone who can ride in the beginner's classes and get some points for us."

Then she turned to me and explained. "Mom's talking about the show between the Shadow Hills Club and Greenway Stables. That's us. It's held every year in September, just before we go back to school. Shadow Hills is this ritzy riding academy. All the kids there have their own horses and grooms and trainers and everything that it takes to win at the big horse shows. And mostly that's what they stick to, the big shows. But a long time ago, so long ago that no one really remembers how it all started, the owners of the two stables got together and decided it would be fun to have an annual horse show. And they figured out a kind of point system so that the kids who didn't have a lot of things, like super-trained horses and grooms, would have a chance to win too. But so far we haven't had enough kids to compete in all the classes. So we haven't been able to get enough points to win because of that. Especially older kids that are in the beginners' classes. Wow! Wouldn't it be fantastic if you could clean up in those!"

And then I could see she was getting all bouncy inside so naturally I smiled back and said, "Yeh, it sure would." But inside I was beginning to get that trapped feeling. I could see they took their riding pretty seriously. What was I getting myself into? All I'd wanted was to meet some kids so I wouldn't be lonely for the summer.

Mrs. Hunter's voice broke into my thoughts. "It really is quite an exciting show. There's a large silver trophy the town businessmen donated some years ago, too. That stays with the winning team for the year. It's lovely."

"Who'd know!" I looked at Tamara's face and it was clouded for the first time since I'd met her. But that went right away and a look of determination took its place. "We're going to win it this year or know the reason why. We all vowed we are going to spend every minute of the summer practicing."

She turned to me. "You can see we're pretty serious about the whole thing." (What did I just say?) "So, Boo, if you do take lessons you simply have to mean it because we need every point we can get." She hit me on the knee, then, for emphasis. And her mother took her eyes off the road for a second and turned in my direction and gave me this great big promotional smile and nodded emphatically. Then she was back to the business of driving again. Maybe she preferred to sit and watch, but if her daughter wanted someone to get involved in something she was there to give any added boost that was needed.

"Here we are!"

Mrs. Hunter had turned into a dirt road that bumped over a grassy field toward a clump of white buildings. They looked like they were about two city blocks away. Dust swirled up around us for a couple of minutes and then settled again as the car stopped.

Where we'd ended up was in a large open area. To my left, past Mrs. Hunter's hairdo, I could see a ring made of white fencing with a small, covered grandstand on one side. All around the inside of the ring were a lot of different kinds of obstacles for horses to jump over. There were wooden gates and wooden boxes painted to look like brick walls and hedges, and, of all things, a railroad crossing. (Who the heck would jump a horse over a railroad crossing?)

In front of us, through the windshield, I could see a huge white barn with green trim. There were two doors in the front through which I could see rows of stalls with horses' heads poking out of the upper half of dutch doors. Alongside the barn was an area of fenced squares, like miniature pastures. Each small pasture had a place for eating and a barrel for drinking water. Horses were in some of these, one or two to each square. Apparently it was to be on one of those horses that I was about to agree to spend my summer, or a major portion of it at least.

Through the window on Tamara's side of the car was a neat little frame house, also white with green trim. It had a matching white picket fence around the front of it, which I guessed was meant to keep the horses from stomping all over the lawn. In back of us was the grassy field over which we had just driven.

This had jumps in it too. But unlike the ones in the ring these were made of more permanent stuff, like stacked logs and that sort of thing.

All over the place there were kids busy doing any number of things. There were kids my own age and some Jonathan's age and some older, who, I was sure, were at least seniors in high school. They all looked like they knew what they were doing; and what they were doing they seemed to be extremely competent at doing. I started to get that squiggly feeling again in my stomach. But it didn't have time to develop very far because Tamara was pulling at my arm and telling me to come on because she wanted to introduce me to Mr. Sikes before it was time for her class.

She was out of the car and standing there waiting. Mrs. Hunter was putting the car in gear, telling us to have a good day and that she would see us later on that afternoon. There was nothing to do but to tell her "thank you" for the ride and follow Tamara, who was off almost immediately after waving good-by to her mother.

I raced after her as she raced after a tall, slim man with a thatch of grey hair who was walking toward a very large and extremely nervous looking brownish-colored horse tied to a fence rail near the ring. Tamara called to the man. But the yard was noisy and she had to call a second time before she could get his attention. I had caught up to her by then and she grabbed my arm again and pulled me along until we were all standing together near the horse—much too near the horse, as far as I was concerned. I edged away. The man gave me a kind of funny look and I was sure that he could tell I didn't like horses and didn't want anything to do with them. But that was only for a second and then he smiled. His smile was all white teeth and you could tell right off that it was a real smile. The skin of his face was like old leather and when he smiled the leather broke into about a thousand creases. Above all those creases were these incredibly dark blue eyes that smiled in agreement with his teeth. I liked him right away and suddenly I didn't want him to know I didn't like horses. I don't know why, it just seemed important at the time. So I edged just a little closer and pretended that I had lost my balance before, when I was moving away from his horse.

Tamara introduced us and told him that I had just moved into town and was now her new next-door neighbor—"wasn't that super"—and that I wanted to start taking lessons as soon as possible. (Boy, when she decided someone was going to do something, that was it!)

Mr. Sikes put a hand on Tamara's shoulder and said, "Whoa!" Just like he probably would have to that nervous horse if he had to. "I'm glad you have such a nice new neighbor," and here he smiled again. "But maybe she isn't all that excited about learning to ride. Then again, maybe she is. In any case, why don't you let Boo and me do the talking about any lessons she might want to take. And we'll do that

after class. Because right now you are late, young lady, and if I stop to talk now I'll be late too. So why don't you go and tell Mrs. Sikes that you're here and then get your horse and go on into the ring and warm up until the class is ready to start."

Tamara did some bouncing in place, half wanting to stay and organize my future and half wanting to hurry and get ready for her class. Then she said, "OK, Mr. Sikes." And she looked at me and said, "Gotta go, see ya after class." Then she was chasing off toward the place where they had all the horses outside the barn.

"It was my fault she was late, Mr. Sikes. That's because I was late getting to her house and she waited for me. I'm sorry."

Mr. Sikes had untied the horse and was now holding him by the reins. "Don't worry, Boo. She isn't really late. I just wanted to stop her before she had you committed to riding in the National Horse Show. She gets carried away with her enthusiasm. Not that I mind it. I like Tamara a lot. She's one of my best riders. It's just that she doesn't understand that not everyone feels the same way about riding that she does. I'll tell you what. Why don't you go on over to the grandstand and watch this class? Then afterward we can talk. I'll tell you what the beginning lessons are like and you can make up your own mind." He smiled again, and turned to get on his horse.

I said, "Thank you, I will," but I wasn't sure that he'd heard me. He must have, though, because after he was up on the horse and adjusting his reins he looked down at me and very gravely said, "You are most welcome." Then he winked and turned the horse around so it was heading toward the ring. He looked over his shoulder in an afterthought and said, "There's a soft drink machine over near the office in case you get thirsty." Then before I could say anything else he nudged the horse with his heels and trotted into the ring.

I decided I was thirsty and looked around for the office. At first I didn't see anything that looked like one, but then I noticed an opening, like a large window, on the side of the house that was closest to the barn and what looked like a large red refrigerator standing near it. I walked across and I was right. I put a quarter in the slot, got a Coke, and pulled the ring tab and dropped it into the little slot on the front of the machine that said "put tabs here." Then I walked across the yard and climbed into the grandstand. All the while I was thinking, Mr. Sikes understands that I might not want to take riding lessons but I don't think he understands the choice is not so simple as whether I want to or don't want to but rather whether I want to make friends this summer. That's the choice. "But come on now, Boo," I said to myself, nearly out loud. "It isn't all that bad. Maybe riding will be fun after all."

It was nice and cool in the shade of the grandstand. The kids were all in the class now and trotting around and bouncing (later I learned this was called posting

and was intentional) up and down to the horse's
motion. They did this for a while going one way and
then everyone changed direction and went the other
way. After that they all lined up in the center, on
either side of the judge's stand, and started taking
turns going over the jumps.

I leaned on my knees and drank some of my Coke
and started thinking. That trotting around didn't look
too hard and I didn't really think you could get too
hurt just doing that. But jumping, now that was
definitely something else to consider. That was where
I was going to draw the line. I didn't think I ever
wanted to have anything to do with that. And anyone
who did was just plain crazy.

"They're crazy!"

I jumped about a foot and almost spilled Coke
down the front of my purple and white T-shirt. Did I
say that out loud? Was I so out of it that I really was
talking to myself? Then I heard it again.

"They are crazy! Anyone who gets on a stupid
horse and jumps over a stupid jump is crazy!"

Then I realized that the voice was coming from
somewhere over on my right. I looked in that direction and saw a girl of about eight with brown braids
and dirty white T-shirt that was miles too big on her
and had printed in red ink across the front, TAKE ME
I'M YOURS.

Silently I agreed with her but thought it best not to
express my opinion in words that might be traced
back to me. So I said, "Don't you like horses?"

"Oh, I like horses all right, to pet and to watch in parades and in Western movies, but that's about as far as I go on the subject of horses." She moved a little closer so that we had eye contact. "Do you like horses?"

"Of course!" Now why had I been as definite as all that? In defense I said, "If you don't like horses very much, then why are you here?"

"Because of him." And she pointed a grubby finger at someone sitting out in the center of the ring on the horse next to the one Tamara was riding. Tamara and this someone were talking together and laughing and all I could see was a bit of chin and some nose under the visor of his riding hat.

"Who's he?"

"He's my brother."

"Oh," I said, not understanding much more than I did in the beginning.

"I have to stay with him because my parents both work and it's cheaper than hiring a full-time sitter. Besides, I'm really too old for a sitter, but I'm not old enough to stay alone all day. According to my mother, that is."

"Oh," I said again. Not knowing what else to say. Then, because I didn't just want to stare at her, with all that eye contact and such, I looked out at her brother again. It was his turn to take the jumps now. I watched him and he did it very well. In fact awfully well. And I realized as he passed in front of the grandstand that he was cute, too. It could be that riding lessons had their good side after all. But then I noticed that when he had finished he went back to where Tamara was. I noticed too that they seemed awfully chummy. I wanted more information.

"Let me get you a Coke," I said.

5

Between the time I bought Deborah Horton (that's her name) a Coke and the time the class ended I had learned:

a) a lot about Deborah,

b) that she has a pet frog named Algernon,

c) an Irish terrier named Andrew, and

d) twin cousins who live in Akron, Ohio.

But about the only information I pried out of her in relation to her brother Troy (that's his name) was:

a) he always opens cereal boxes at the wrong end so he can get the prize without having to eat the cereal, and

b) nine times out of ten he is to be found wearing socks that don't match because he never can find two clean ones that do.

So much for sophisticated bribery. What I had wanted to find out was:

a) his opinion of girls in general, and

b) his opinion of Tamara in particular.

Well, as Confucius, or someone, once said, "If you want something done well, do it yourself." Obviously, I was going to have to find these things out for myself.

If he and Tamara were a duo, it was hands off, absolutely. Because, though I haven't yet (as I've stated before) had any great experience in the way of boys, I do know from watching other relationships between friends that the interruption of a boy-girl relationship by a third party sometimes leads to the third party becoming an outcast. And I didn't want to become an "out" before I became an "in"—if you know what I mean.

However, if there wasn't a boy-girl relationship between the two of them, then it might definitely be to my advantage to find out more about him than that his socks don't match and he likes the prizes in the bottoms of cereal boxes.

Oh, I know that boys aren't everything, and the world is not going to come to an end if you don't have a boyfriend. Nevertheless, since Mom's law is that I can start dating when I'm fourteen, and since I am going to be fourteen in a few more months, there is no harm in doing some serious thinking along that line, is there?

Right this minute, however, my boy-type thinking was going to have to wait. The class had ended and

Mr. Sikes had ridden over to the edge of the grand-stand and was sitting there on his horse, shielding his eyes from the sun, and looking up into the stand.

"Boo, are you up there?"

"Yes, Mr. Sikes. Here I am." And I got up and went down to the bottom of the stand so that he could see me.

"If you'd like to talk about those lessons now I can meet you in the office just as soon as I put Jeep away. Why don't you go over there now." Then he raised his hand in a little wave and was off.

"You'll be sorry!" came a jeer from behind me. I'd almost forgotten about Deborah, girl horse-hater. I turned, looked back up into the stand, shrugged my shoulders, and said, "We'll see!"

To my retreating back she yelled, "Don't worry, I'll be here to catch you when you hit the ground." Then she laughed as only an eight-year-old brat, who's pretty sure of where she stands, can laugh.

The office was actually the Sikes's kitchen, a big comfortable room that held not only the kitchen table but a desk and several easy chairs of various vintages and styles. Mr. Sikes had not yet arrived but Mrs. Sikes was there. She smiled a smile that was like Mr. Sikes's smile in that it was real and motioned me to a chair with a hand that was full of hamburger meat.

I sat down and smiled back at her. She was busy forming patties and piling them on a plate. There were an awful lot of them and I was wondering who she was making them for. She saw my look and explained.

"They're for lunch. I make hamburgers, or something like that, every day for the kids who are taking lessons. After all, they're here all day and there's not too many places to go to eat near here." She shook her head. "Kids being kids, either they won't bring a lunch from home or they forget to. Anyway, a couple of summers ago I started making lunch for everybody. I was already feeding half of them anyway. They do pay. There's a kitty and everyone puts in money for the month. You can do the same if you decide to take lessons. We're all kind of one big family. It's only natural that families eat together, right?" She smiled and started making patties again.

I felt a little awkward just sitting there and I'm sure she realized it because pretty soon she went over to the sink and came back with a bowl of tomatoes and a knife and said, "Here, why don't you slice these for me."

She finished forming the patties and put them on a big grill. They sizzled, and the smell made me realize how hungry I was.

"Your name is Boo," she said. "I know because your mother called a little while ago to get some information about the lessons and how much they cost. She told me to tell you that if you want to go ahead and sign up it would be fine with her."

Mr. Sikes came in the door while I was still busy cutting and stacking slices of tomatoes on a large plate. "Looks like you've joined the crew." He leaned against the counter and chuckled softly. "But, then, Mrs. Sikes has a way of recruiting people without their being aware of it. You're naturally welcome to be a member of the kitchen crew anytime you'd like. But, now, what I'd like to find out is how you feel about those lessons."

I'd just about finished up on the tomatoes and Mrs. Sikes took the knife away from me and said to go ahead and talk to Mr. Sikes as horses were a lot more important than tomatoes any day.

I looked at Mr. Sikes and was about to say that I had made up my mind and that I wanted to take lessons, but he stopped me before I could say a word.

"Before you commit yourself I'd like to tell you something about how I operate, because, I think, Greenway Stables is very much different from any other stables you've ever been to."

So what did I know of any other stable? Over the next fifteen minutes, though, I certainly learned a lot about Greenway. I found out that Mr. Sikes felt strongly about riding being a two-way affair and that, as far as he was concerned, sitting on a horse well was only part of being a good horsewoman. So half of his lessons were given on the ground learning about how the horse thought and acted and how to take care of it, and the other half were given on the horses. As for the horses, Mr. Sikes assigned one to each rider to be his or hers for every lesson. No one else rode that horse, so it was almost like having your own. The one rub was that you had to take care of that horse as if it were your own as well. You even had to clean out its stall. That was important, too.

Mrs. Sikes broke in then and said the hamburgers were done and wouldn't I prefer to eat mine with the other kids. She smiled at me in a conspiratorial manner as if she knew that I was a bit overwhelmed by all this and wanted some more time to think about things. She handed me a hamburger wrapped in waxed paper, a bag of potato chips, and a carton of milk and pointed out the window to an area under a big tree where there were some redwood picnic tables.

Tamara was already seated at one of the tables and was waving at me to come over to where she had a place saved. At the table were Troy and Deborah and two other kids. I slipped in between Tamara and a red-faced boy with sandy-colored hair. Troy was sitting on the other side of Tamara.

"Boo, this is Troy Horton," said Tamara. "He's one of the best riders we have."

"Hi!" said Troy.

"And this is Grant Hillard," Tamara gestured toward the red-faced boy on my right. "He just started riding about six months ago so he isn't too much ahead of you." Grant had his mouth full of hamburger and was stuffing a stray piece of onion into it, but he nodded vigorously in my direction.

"And this is Sally Gunther." Sally was sitting across from me. "Her dad owns the feed store and donates a lot of the ribbons for the show that we *hope* we are going to win this year." The word hope was stressed and she looked in my direction when she said it.

Sally said, "Hi!" I noticed her mouth was full of metal. I felt for her. It hadn't been too long ago that I had had a mouthful of railroad tracks myself.

"And this is Debbie Horton, Troy's younger sister." The way she said the name you knew there was no love lost but that Tamara didn't want Troy to know that.

"My name is *Deborah,* not Debbie," said Deborah through clenched teeth with an attitude that meant the feeling was strictly mutual. Then she looked at me. "Did you get the royal lecture?"

"Come on, Deborah, stuff it," her brother said. "Just because you don't like horses doesn't mean other people don't."

Deborah made a sour face and sucked noisily at her straw.

Once the introductions had been made everyone got down to the business of eating. Halfway through the meal two other kids joined us. Their names were Bob and Dennis Weiner. They were older. They acted it, too, but they were still friendly and seemed like a part of the group. I guess if everyone's interested in the same thing, age doesn't make all that much difference.

I had just put the last bite of my hamburger in my mouth when Troy asked me what horse Mr. Sikes had given me. Terrific timing, I thought, pointing toward my full mouth and making idiot nodding motions.

Tamara jumped into the middle of my munching and said, "I bet it's Big Dan. His leg's just about healed up."

"Nope, it's gotta be Atta Baby," said Sally. "Mr. Sikes said Big Dan needs another ten days of rest, and Atta Baby is free now that Alicia has moved to Lynchburg."

"You're both wrong. I think I'll give her Graham Cracker." Everyone looked up and there was Mr. Sikes leaning against a tree chuckling. Boy! He could be an Indian scout any day.

"Graham Cracker!!!" That was Tamara, Troy, and Sally all speaking at once. "You've got to be kidding."

"Now you know I never kid when it comes to horses. When I said Graham Cracker, I meant Graham Cracker. So when you've finished lunch why don't you three nonbelievers take Boo down and introduce her to him. That is, if Boo has decided about those lessons."

"Of course she has!" said Tamara, taking no chances on any negative answer from me. "Let's go right now. Wow! I don't believe it! Graham Cracker!"

And I was off to meet Graham Cracker.

6

"Boo . . . HELP!!"

I fought my way through a tangle of chairs, coffee tables, rolled rugs, table lamps, and a sectional sofa and arrived in the kitchen door to find Mom perched with one foot on the kitchen counter and the other on the back of a kitchen chair. She was trying to push a heavy carton full of junk onto the top of a cabinet over her head. The chair had started to slide over the slippery vinyl floor toward the center of the kitchen so that Mom now looked as if she were trying out for a gymnastics team.

"My heavens, Boo! Don't just stand there. I'm about to be turned into two people. Push the chair! Push the chair!!"

I got behind the chair and heaved and pushed and pretty soon Mom was back to an upright position.

She shoved the carton onto the ledge, then squatted down and swung her legs out, and sat down on the top of the counter.

"I don't know, Boo. Sometimes I think you're right about moving. I really do hate all this unpacking. I don't know where to put everything. Look at this kitchen! It was built for a family of one. There's no room to put anything anywhere! And the living room. I didn't think we had that much furniture, but we do, and I just can't decide where to put it all."

Right here I would like to explain briefly that this is the normal reaction from Mom, and it occurs each time we move. And each time, before we move, I remind her about how it's going to be, hoping that she will cancel any and all thoughts about moving. But it never works. So, instead of all the sympathy that you think I should be showing, and which I would if this weren't something that happened every year, I calmly said, "Mom, I'm sorry about the kitchen and I'm sorry about the living room and I'm sorry about there being too much furniture. But, and here's the big BUT . . . all this wouldn't be a problem if we would just stop moving around. You wouldn't have to almost kill yourself trying to put a box of junk up on a shelf—junk that you probably aren't even going to touch until the next time we move. And our furniture wouldn't get worn out with trying to fit it into different houses and—"

"You can stop right there, Boo. I think I know this speech by heart." She shut up then and sat swinging her legs and looking as though she was having some kind of an argument inside of herself. "I know you're right. And maybe someday we will stop moving. Maybe this time things will be right. I don't know."

Then she jumped down from the counter, dusted her hands on the backsides of her jeans, and smiled briefly. "Maybe. Just maybe! But right now I do have to figure out where to put all that stuff in the living room. And I need you to help me push the furniture around."

"OK, Mom," I said. "And listen, I'm sorry I blew off at the mouth. I didn't mean to make you feel guilty about it, or anything. It's just that I really do want to stay put sometime. Do you understand?"

"Yes, Boo. I do understand." And for a minute that unhappy look was back and I was sorry that I'd said that thing about feeling guilty, because I know she really does feel guilty about moving us about so much. And underneath I think I understand why she feels she has to move so often. I think Mom is looking for something she hasn't been able to find yet—a way of life, people she can be friends with—I don't really know what it is, but it's something like that, I'm sure. And realizing that makes me realize that grownups sometimes have the same problems that kids do and that there are some problems that don't go away just because you get older.

Then, because I was feeling a little guilty myself for having accused her of feeling guilty, I wanted to make her forget that I'd brought the whole thing up. "Hey,

Mom, I've got an idea. Why don't we go and get some pizza? While we're eating we can draw up some of those little diagrams that you make when you're trying to decorate a room. That way we can decide where to put the furniture and when we get back from eating we can just zing right into it. We'll have the living room all finished and ready in case anyone comes over to visit."

"Boo," she smiled hugely. "That is one terrific idea! Fact is, I am absolutely starved." Then she put her arms around me and gave me a big bear hug and kissed the top of my head. "I think that's why I love you so much. Because you have such terrific ideas! Now go get Jonathan. Tell him he can run rampant at the salad bar. I'll try and find my purse under all this gunk and meet you out in the car."

The pizza was good. Lots of sausage, green peppers, black olives, and onions, just the way I like it. That and two large Cokes just about did me in. I think it had the same effect on Mom. (Jonathan doesn't count. I mean, how much can a bowl of lettuce affect you?) But after all the unpacking we'd done, without stopping since early this morning, we had a right to be pooped. So when we got home from the pizza parlor, instead of moving the furniture, we each looked for a piece that was free of boxes and stuff and flaked out.

By the time we started stirring around again it was nearly five o'clock in the afternoon. Mom looked around and said, "The heck with doing anything in the living room today. The furniture's not going to go anywhere. It'll wait until tomorrow. Instead why don't you and Jonathan go unpack some of your own things so you can at least find your beds by tonight."

I can't tell you how glad I was that Mom had made that decision. I hate falling asleep during the daytime because when I do wake up I feel worse than when I went to sleep. Not only am I still tired, but I feel all puffy and rumpled as well. All I want to do is go back to sleep. Which was exactly what I planned to do as soon as I got up to my room.

I followed Jonathan upstairs and then went into my own room. Mine was on the back corner of the house and the windows overlooked our backyard as well as Tamara's and the two houses that back up to ours, on the next street over. I liked that. I like seeing what's going on.

Mom always lets Jonathan and me have the pick of the bedrooms. Jonathan usually gets the master bedroom because he has all this paraphernalia that a budding scientist is supposed to have. Maybe that would seem strange to a lot of adults but Mom says, to her, it seems silly for the grownups, who don't have half the stuff that kids usually do, to get to use the big bedroom and stick the kids in a room the size of an overgrown closet.

I always look for a room that is different. I don't care about size. My room in California had a bay window with a window seat that doubled as storage space. (You remember the near tragedy when I almost lost Big Blue!)

The room I picked out in this house had a fire-place—a real one. It was a tiny Victorian kind with an opening like a half circle and a white plaster border all around that had cupids and vines and flowers molded on it. A mantle was above it that stuck out on each side so that it made a shelf along the width of the room.

I looked at this mantle and suddenly wondered how my stuffed animals would look on it. I forgot all about going back to sleep and started hunting through cartons marked "Boo's room—books," "Boo's room—pillows," "Boo's room—pictures" until I found the one marked "Boo's room—inanimate creatures." (Jonathan had had the job of marking the boxes.) I dusted off the shelf, using a stray pajama bottom I'd found in among the stuffed animals. Then I arranged them all so that they looked comfortable and at home.

Two years before, Mom had found a little bedroom chair at a garage sale and, in a fit of domesticity, had covered it in dark pink chintz to go with my pink and white gingham spread and curtains. I pulled this over so that it sat on one side of the fireplace. Then the bed, which the movers had left pushed up against the wall, looked all wrong so I moved some boxes away from between the two windows and shoved it between them with the foot of the bed sticking out into the room. I wondered if the curtains would fit. I scrambled through the cartons again until I found them, stuffed down among the books along with the spread. They were clean but all wrinkled. I sure didn't want to hang them up that way, so I went downstairs to get the iron and the ironing board.

Mom was back in the kitchen. She was putting in shelf paper and humming to herself. She stopped humming and said, "Hi! How're you doing?"

"Hey," I said companionably, "I think my room's going to be OK." I got the iron and the board and headed back up the stairs.

The curtains fit, almost, and after I'd put on the spread, which wasn't wrinkled because it is quilted, and hung up the curtains, I was beginning to feel at home. It's funny how little things that are familiar will do that.

In another spurt of activity I unpacked the rest of my stuff, putting away books in the bookcase that was on the same side of the fireplace as the chair, and arranging my collection of glass owls on the dresser. As the cartons became empty I stacked them outside the door, and everything that I couldn't find a place for I piled in the center of the room. When I'd emptied all the boxes, and all that was left was the pile of miscellaneous objects, I opened the closet door and shoved the pile inside and closed the door. Things were now back to normal. I stood there for a full minute admiring my handywork before the disaster struck.

All at once a noise, like that of a maddened rhinoceros charging through a swamp, came from the other side of my bedroom door. When I opened it, there was Jonathan attacking the boxes I had so neatly stacked. He was throwing them every which way, all over the upstairs hall. For a minute I couldn't believe my eyes. Quiet, placid, dignified Jonathan was behaving like the wild man from Borneo.

"Just what is going on?" I asked. "Are you out of your tree? Has the Virginia air fried your brain?"

Jonathan looked up at me then and I could see that his face was twisted all funny and his eyes were squinty and watery looking, as if he wanted to cry but wasn't sure how to. "I can't find Wentworth. He's gone. He isn't anyplace."

"Hey, hold it, troop! What do you mean Wentworth's gone? He can't have gotten very far. Good grief, he's so fat he can barely move and would probably need a taxi to get to the next room. Now, calm down and tell me where all you've looked."

Then, before he could tell me, Mom stuck her head around the corner of the staircase and wanted to know what all the racket was about. Jonathan wailed an answer, and I translated it. Then Mom came upstairs and took charge. She managed to get Jonathan calmed down a bit and we learned that he had pretty much searched the second floor.

There is no doubt in my mind that Jonathan is thorough, and I was sure he had covered the territory well. But we looked again, just the same. Then the search moved downstairs and we were pretty thorough there, too. We even checked the backyard with the aid of a flashlight because it was dark by then. But no luck.

I have never, in all my life, seen Jonathan this upset. And I thought about how I'd felt about Big Blue the time we left him, and how I'd said I'd even walk back all that way to get him. Jonathan was sitting on the stairs with his head in his hands. He was quiet, but every once in a while I could see a tear fall on the carpet. I sat down next to him and put my arm around his shoulders. I didn't say anything though, because I couldn't think of anything that would make things seem any better.

But mothers are supposed to know what to say at times like these. There seems to be some kind of unwritten law. I looked up at her and I could see that she was definitely upset. But it was more because of the way Jonathan was taking this than that Wentworth was missing.

"Jonathan, darling, I'm sure that Wentworth is someplace here in the house and that we just haven't discovered where yet. I really don't think he could have gone very far. What I think happened is that he didn't like all the noise the moving men were making and found a quiet place for a nap. Probably by morning he'll wake up and find out that everything is quiet again and come out of hiding."

She tried on a reassuring smile, but Jonathan didn't even look up and she soon dropped it.

"No. You're wrong. He's gone. He's gone, and he's never going to come back." Jonathan said that very quietly. And I knew that he was desperately unhappy.

I looked up at Mom. But she just sighed and looked back at me and I could tell she felt that way too. She wasn't the only one. I, too, had a feeling that Jonathan was right—Wentworth *was* gone.

7

Wentworth was still missing.

Mom got me up early, and together we searched the house and garden again, being quiet so that we wouldn't wake up Jonathan, and hoping against hope that Wentworth would miraculously appear.

But he didn't.

We were busy searching the last of the moving cartons, which were stacked in the downstairs hall, and whispering to each other and tiptoeing about and shushing no one in particular whenever something fell over or went bang . . . when we heard Jonathan's voice from somewhere above us.

"I told you he was gone!"

We looked up and there he was, sitting on the top of the stairs. He had his head in his hands again, but at least this time he wasn't crying.

"Jonathan, stop it!" Mom said, just a little too sharply, and I knew she hadn't changed her mind about how she really thought. "We haven't looked everywhere. After all, with this furniture stacked every which way, it wasn't possible to look in every spot where he might be. So, now that you're up I am going to fix us some breakfast and then, after we eat, we can get busy and move the furniture. We might just discover that he has been hiding here in the living room all this time."

I don't know what it is about mothers. But in a time of crisis they almost always turn to food as an answer to the problem, or at least a temporary solution. Probably it's because mothers spend so much time in the kitchen dealing with food that to them it is the most obvious tactic.

Whatever, I was glad that it was this tactic Mom had chosen. First because I was hungry and awfully tired of looking for that stupid snake. And second because I did want to get Jonathan off those stairs and stop him from looking so glum. So Mom was probably right in suggesting food. For if there is any person that is a munchmouth, it is Jonathan. He may be a vegetarian and a health freak, but that sure doesn't stop him from stuffing himself ninety-four hours a day.

"Come on, Jonathan," I said. "Mom's getting breakfast and I think we ought to go eat it." I stood there staring at him until he finally got up and dragged himself down the stairs. Then we went into the kitchen.

I had finished my second helping of scrambled eggs and sausages when I looked over and noticed that Mom had barely touched her breakfast. When I looked at Jonathan's plate it was still piled high with fruit and he'd only taken one bite out of his sprouted-wheat muffin.

For a moment I felt like an unfeeling glutton. But then I thought to myself, "Nonsense, Boo! You're a growing girl and you need all those calories. After all, you're going to have to push that furniture all around. And then there's your first riding lesson this morning. . . ." Oh, my gosh! I'd almost forgotten all about my riding lesson. Tamara's mother was driving again this morning and Tamara had stressed the point about my not being late again today. I looked at the clock and it was ten minutes after nine already.

"Hey, Mom. I don't want to seem unconcerned or anything, but could we get that furniture moved? I have to be ready to leave in about forty-five minutes."

"Oh, sure, Boo." She put the fork down she'd been toying with. "Come on. We'll do it right now."

We'd finally shoved the last chair into place, and there wasn't any place left in the living room where Wentworth could possibly be hiding. I looked at Mom and she shrugged her shoulders and looked defeated. I was searching for something to suggest when I heard someone calling from outside the screen door in the kitchen.

It was Tamara. I couldn't hear exactly what she was saying, but I didn't need to. I looked at the grandfather clock in the hall and it was ten minutes after ten. I yelled something about being almost ready and to meet me out in front. Jonathan was still sitting in the kitchen, staring at his papaya, and I didn't want Tamara getting anywhere near him so that he could relate his sad tale of woe to her. All that was needed to set off an international (or at least interneighborhood) incident was for Tamara to find out that Wentworth was loose somewhere . . . possibly even in her very own backyard.

I checked my pocket for the check that Mom had written out earlier for the lessons, stuck my hair brush in the back pocket of my jeans, and kissed Mom while mumbling something about being sorry, but I had to go.

She smiled weakly and said, "Thanks, Boo. I love you too. Have a good time."

I went out the front door and down to where Tamara was now waiting.

"Hi!" I said. "Sorry, I didn't realize what time it was. I was helping Mom with the living-room furniture. You know how it is!"

"Yeh, I know. Well, let's go. I don't want to be too late!" I detected a slight bit of annoyance and I silently vowed I was never, never going to be late again when it came to going anywhere with Tamara.

Her mother leaned over and said, "Good morning, Boo." Then, just as I was getting into the car, she said, "Where's your hat, dear?"

Then Tamara looked at me and her eyes were just slightly squinty when she said, "Where *is* your hat?"

My hat! Oh, great. I'd forgotten all about my hat. In fact I wasn't really sure about where it was. It could have gone down some black hole, the way Wentworth went, as far as I knew. (I know. By now you're wondering, what hat? Well, it seems that when you ride a horse you are supposed to wear this kind of hard hat that keeps you from splitting your head open in case you fall off the horse. And at Greenway it is absolutely required. No hat—no horse. Mr. Sikes had equipped me with one when I'd signed up for the lessons day before yesterday.) Now, where the heck was it? I'd brought it back to the motel. But what happened to it after that?

To Tamara and Mrs. Hunter I said, "Oh, how dumb of me. I must have left it on the kitchen counter. I'll be right back." And I tore off around the back of our house and into the kitchen and past Jonathan and into the living room where Mom was sitting, forlornly, on the couch.

"Mom! My hat! My hat! I don't know where it is. I've got to have it. Tamara and her mother are out in their car absolutely having fits because we are already late. And I told them I knew where it was and that I'd be right back. But I don't know where it is. Do you?"

"Oh, Boo!" Mom sighed. "What next? Can't anybody keep track of their own things? Now, look. It has to be someplace in your room. I put all of your clothes and your suitcase from the motel up in your room when we came over here yesterday morning. So it must be there. Besides, we've searched the rest of the house and we'd have run across it if it had been any other place but in your room. I know you haven't had time to start stuffing things under your bed. And I don't think you could squeeze one more thing into any drawer of your dresser. So it must be either on the mantle, the top of your bookcase, or on the bottom of your closet . . . and I'm willing to bet that is where it is. Now, why don't you go and see!"

"Genius, Mom . . . pure genius! Thanks!" And I was on my way up the stairs to my room.

It was not on the bookcase. And it was not on the mantle. I opened the closet and started pulling out various objects from the pile on the floor. It was there, underneath everything, a little black-velvet bowl, full of—

WENTWORTH . . .

Now, Wentworth and I have never been the greatest of friends. I don't really like snakes. But I sure was glad to see him this time. I grabbed the hat and went racing downstairs to where Mom was.

"Look . . . look . . . look! Here he is! He was sleeping in my hat. I guess we didn't see him because the hat's black and he's black and the inside of my closet is pretty black and—"

"And probably because no one thought to look there," Mom finished up for me. "Oh, thank heaven! . . . Jonathan. . . . Jonathan!"

But there was no need to call his name a third time. He was in and gathering Wentworth up in his arms and hugging him. (Can you hug a snake?)

BOO! ARE YOU COMING, OR NOT?"

That was Tamara.

"I'm coming . . . right now!"

That was me.

Jonathan was blubbering and laughing and hugging Wentworth. And it was a side of Jonathan I still wasn't used to.

"I'm glad he's back, troop." I said to him.

"Me, too!" said Jonathan. "Thanks for finding him."

"OK, but no more naps in my hat, huh?" And I rumpled Jonathan's hair . . . an act I would ordinarily never think of performing. Then I went on out to join Tamara and her mother and try to make peace.

8

I learned several things during my first lesson.
I learned that when you lead a horse, or get on him, you do it from the left side. And that this left side is called the "near" side. The other side is called the "off" side. It's sort of like port and starboard when you are on a boat.

I learned how to put the saddle on and the bridle, and which goes on first. It's the saddle.

I learned that you always groom your horse before you ride and that it is very important to look at the bottom of his feet to see if there is anything there that might make him lame. I don't like doing this as it involves getting much too close to a part of the horse that can hurt you.

I learned, too, that as long as I am having to take lessons, I'm glad that Mr. Sikes decided to give me Graham Cracker.

Tamara and Troy and Sally, however, do not share my opinion. They think that my being given Graham Cracker is absolutely horrible and that I should at least be upset, if not humiliated, by the choice.

"Honestly, Boo! Don't you understand?" Tamara was stuffed full of indignity. "How can you even consider riding that silly beast?"

Sally was not as volatile as Tamara, but her opinion was in the same vein. "Mr. Sikes has gone completely bananas!"

Troy was on the line. I could tell he wanted to defend Mr. Sikes's decision, but that he couldn't understand it any more than Tamara or Sally. "I don't know . . . Mr. Sikes doesn't make mistakes very often. Although I sure think he made one this time. But, Tamara, I don't think you should call Cracker a silly beast. After all, you learned on him and so did Sally and so did I. And we all loved him. And we all still do—at least I do. So don't take your feelings out on him. All right!"

"That isn't the point and you know it, Troy!" Tamara was still indignant. "We were just kids when we learned to ride. You don't put someone Boo's age on a pony . . . the very idea . . . *a pony!*"

And that was how I learned that Graham Cracker was a pony. Because, up until they exploded all over the place like that, I didn't even know that he was a pony.

Hold it. . . .

Before you start doubling up and rolling on the floor over the idea too, and wondering how on earth it was that I couldn't even tell a pony when I saw one, let me explain.

Not all ponies are those fat little things that kids pay fifty cents to ride on at a carnival. Un-uh! They come in assorted sizes. And a lot of them look just like regular horses, only they aren't quite so tall. And, as I learned later, on the East Coast—of which Virginia is a part—it is perfectly proper to ride and show a pony clear up until you are thirteen, and sometimes fourteen.

But that's when you *stop* riding ponies—not start. And that's what Tamara and Sally and Troy were so uptight about. And Tamara was all set to go and see Mr. Sikes and make him give me a real, to quote her, horse to ride.

But I stopped her. Maybe it's because I'm so conscious of being short myself that somehow I felt it was unfair to condemn Graham Cracker just because he is two or three inches shorter than the horses they are used to riding. So I said, "Listen, it's my problem. So let me handle it. I'll talk to Mr. Sikes. But not right now."

"All right, Boo! It's your funeral," Tamara sputtered. "But if you get any static, let me know and I'll jump right in."

"Boy, you can bank on that!" Troy said. And Tamara shot him a look that said this wasn't the first time he'd made that kind of crack toward her. That made me think again about what kind of relationship actually did exist between them. I filed the thought away to be mulled over at a later time.

I didn't really have any intention of talking to Mr. Sikes. I didn't care all that much. But he talked to me. In fact, as soon as the others left he came over to where I was standing, near Graham Cracker.

"I see you're friends already. Or at least I can tell that he likes you. See, his ears are pricked forward and he's hoping you have a piece of sugar, or a carrot, to give him. Here." Mr. Sikes handed me a piece of sugar and showed me how to hold it—flat on the center of my palm so I wouldn't get nipped. It felt funny when Cracker's nose snuffled at my palm and he picked up the sugar. I never realized how soft horses' noses are. Like warm velvet.

"Oh, I like him OK, but—"

"I know. Tamara and Troy and Sally all think you are much too old to ride a pony. Right? Well, it's my guess that you didn't even know Cracker was a pony until they told you. And I'm willing to bet that Cracker doesn't even know he's a pony, either. Furthermore, I think you are too much your own person to let others make up your mind for you. I think you know that what may be right for one person, or even a whole lot of people, is not always what's right for another person. What I'm trying to say is that I had a very good reason for giving you Graham Cracker. But I want you to figure that out for yourself. However, I'll give you a clue. There is an old horseman's saying that I think is pretty wise. I like to try and stick

to it whenever I can, and when I do, things go along just about the way they're supposed to. It goes like this: 'Suit the horse to the rider and the rider to the horse.' Think about it." Then he reached in his pocket and gave me another cube of sugar for Cracker.

I thought I had a pretty good idea about how the rule applied to me but I wasn't positive until after I had finished my first lesson. Then I knew for sure. And I was ready for Mr. Sikes when he came up to me and asked me if I'd figured the reason out yet.

"Uh-huh! I think so. Is it because I'm short and I wouldn't fit a tall horse very well?"

"Dead right, Boo! I knew you were smart . . . almost as smart as Cracker . . . and just as cute, too."

He rode away and I felt good, and warm all over. I thought I understood why all the kids worked so hard for him. He could be stern and very strict when he was teaching a class, but when it was over he made you feel like you were very special. I was glad that I'd figured out the reason he'd given me Cracker, even though it hadn't been all that hard to figure out.

It's funny how most people who don't ride horses—and that certainly included me up until a very short while ago—don't realize that just about as much time is spent on the ground, working with the horse, as on top of him.

You have to groom him and saddle and bridle him, and when your leading him you don't want to feel as though he is towering over you so much that you have no control. Then there's the problem of getting on. If your legs aren't long enough to stretch and reach the stirrup, you're going to have to locate a rock or a box to stand on. And those aren't always handy out in the middle of some grassy field.

So Cracker and I made a pretty good pair, he being a pony-sized horse and I being a pony-sized girl. And it didn't matter to me that he was a pony, for it wasn't as if I was planning on making this riding affair permanent. This was just a summer thing . . . strictly to make friends. As soon as school started in the fall, that was it for horses. And that's for sure!

Something else I learned during that first lesson was that riding involves muscles you never even considered your body had. Even riding at a walk is hard work if you do it properly. You have to keep your heels down and your toes up and turned in, almost as if you were pigeon-toed. Then you have to make your knees go knock-kneed into the saddle so that you're sort of locked in and won't fall off so easily. And, after you have every muscle in your legs screaming "unfair," you have to concentrate on keeping your hands still so you aren't jerking on the reins every time the horse makes a move. Furthermore, your elbows, which you just naturally want to use to keep your balance, have to be tucked neatly in at your sides instead of flapping up and down. And all this time you have to keep your back straight with your eyes looking right between the horse's ears toward where you're going, not down at the rest of you to see if everything's in place.

That's pretty much how the first part of the summer went. As soon as I'd get one set of muscles taken care of and working properly, something new would be added to the lessons and I'd have to start all over again.

But by the middle of August I had accomplished several things. I'd learned how to trot and how to canter and use my reins and hands and legs properly. I could name all the parts of the tack—that's the equipment that goes on the horse, like the bridle and the saddle. And I could nearly name all the parts of the horse. I could muck out a stall in less than ten minutes. I could tell good hay from bad hay.

And I'd learned that Troy does not like Tamara as a girlfriend, even though Tamara thinks he does. This last I learned from Deborah, not Mr. Sikes.

We were sitting in the grandstand one afternoon watching the advanced riders taking a jumping lesson. Tamara and Troy were huddled in the middle of the ring, just as they'd been the first day I'd come to the stable. Suddenly, Deborah made a disgusted noise with her tongue and said, "You'd think she'd get wise sometime, wouldn't you?"

Out of the blue, like that, I wasn't sure of what she was talking about and I said, "Huh?"

"That ding-a-ling, Tamara. Just because she's so hotsy-totsy popular she thinks every boy is going to fall all over her." And she made another sound similar to the first one.

"Oh!"

"Yeh! But that sure doesn't go as far as my brother is concerned. He keeps talking to Tad—that's our older brother who's married and ancient—about it. Tad keeps telling him to go ahead and tell her to get lost. But Troy, like the big stupo he is, says he doesn't want to hurt her precious feelings and wants to stay friends with her. He figures eventually she'll get the message and go find some other guy to zero in on and that probably it'll happen as soon as we get back to school. Frankly, I think he's just putting off doing something that needs doing and isn't going to get any better until it's done." And here she looked at me. "I think somebody, such as a close friend, should tell her the score . . . don't you?"

Well, no person in her right mind is going to commit herself to an answer—in any direction—to a question like that one. And I did consider myself to be in my right mind. So I gave her one of those noncommittal answers that, I hoped, sounded full of wisdom.

"All of us have our own opinions, and you are absolutely right to stand by yours."

Then I left before she had time to figure out that I'd not really said very much of anything. I walked down to the barn to feed Graham Cracker a sugar cube and do a little constructive thinking on my own.

9

Did you ever wish for a long time that you knew the answer to something? And then, when you finally found out, and even though the answer was the one you were hoping for, finding it out didn't solve anything? On the contrary, it made things more complicated.

Well, that was the way it was with me when I found out that Troy didn't really like Tamara as a girlfriend. It's funny. News like that should have made me deliriously happy, knowing that I might have a chance to be the one that Troy liked. But the more I thought about the situation, the more I realized that I wasn't one bit happy.

First of all there was Tamara. Somehow she had deluded herself into thinking that her relationship with Troy had gone past the friendship stage and into the boy-girl stage. How could she have done that? Unless Troy had said something to make her think that. And that made me wonder. About Troy. How could he let Tamara go on thinking that? I mean especially since he likes Tamara as a friend. The whole situation had me bothered. Tamara and Troy had become my closest and dearest friends and I was afraid that if this went on any further one of them was going to get hurt. I no longer wanted Troy as a boyfriend. But I did still want him as a friend. And I wanted Tamara as a friend. And I wanted them both to stay friends with each other. Oh, I tell you. It was a problem. There is no doubt of that. I had to do something about it. Because, sure as heck no one else was going to. You can't really count Deborah. Neither one of them was going to listen to her. Which obviously was why she approached me. But what could I do?

If I told Tamara what I knew, it would make her hate me for knowing it, and that would be the end of our friendship. No one wants to be told that the boy they are positive is their boyfriend is not really their boyfriend. And the person they least want to hear such news from is their best friend. Not rational thinking, I agree, but when you're the injured party and you're confronted with that kind of news, you don't always think rationally.

On the other hand, if I went to Troy and told him I knew how he felt and I thought he should tell Tamara, not only would he hate me for being an interfering snoop, but he would hate me for knowing that he was afraid to tell Tamara how he felt.

Well, I was really stopped dead for an answer. I guess it put me in a frame of mind so that I didn't want to talk to either of them for the rest of the day. I went up to the office and told Mrs. Sikes that I wasn't feeling well and she let me call Mom.

Mom either has awfully good ESP or has learned to read my voice, because she asked me on the phone if I really was sick or just had a problem and wanted to get away from it for a while. I told her she had it figured pretty well, and she said she'd be right out and why didn't I walk out to the main road and meet her there.

I hung up and told Mrs. Sikes it wasn't anything serious, just a little headache and that Mom was coming to pick me up. Then I said I wanted to go ahead and walk out to the main road to just breathe in some fresh air. I told her that so she wouldn't make a fuss and try to get me to lie down or anything. That's always so embarrassing.

No one saw me leave. I walked out to the end of the dirt road and stood there watching the cars come toward me, waiting for one that was blue. It was only about ten minutes before our station wagon came down the road. It stopped and I climbed in and said in a glum voice, "Thanks for picking me up, Mom."

"That's OK, Boo," said Mom. And she drove off. We were silent for a bit. Mom's like that. She doesn't pry or ask questions. But I know I can count on her to listen when, and if, I want to talk about what's bothering me. But I wasn't quite ready to talk yet. I wanted to sort things out for a while longer. So I decided to start a conversation about something neutral to get my mind off the problem and to keep the silence from turning into something uncomfortable.

"Mr. Sikes told us what classes we'd be riding in at the horse show," I said. "Did you realize it's only about ten days away? I'm supposed to ride in a "Beginner's Equitation Class" and a "Hunter Hack Class." Sally told me that I'd have to jump over two jumps in the Hunter Hack Class. But I haven't learned how to jump yet, so I don't understand why Mr. Sikes would put me in that class, do you?"

"My heavens!" said Mom. "Is the show really only ten days away?" She sounded as if she'd misplaced about a month of summer somewhere and hadn't realized it until I'd mentioned it.

When I thought about it, Mom had been pretty busy herself this summer. For the first time since I've known her, which is a pretty long time, she had actually gotten social. By that I mean she had made friends. In fact, Mom and Mrs. Hunter had become almost as good friends as Tamara and I. It was she who'd introduced Mom to her friends and all of a sudden Mom had found herself in the thick of things and loving every minute.

I think the reason for this was that this was the first time we'd ever lived in a small town before. We'd always lived in a big city where you could be neighbors with someone for years and still not even have said hello once. Whatever the reason for the change, I was sure glad. I'd never seen her so happy.

Mom slowed the car to let a dog run across the road. She shifted gears and started up again. Suddenly she said, "That means you should be getting your riding outfit for the show right away. Fact is, that's a good idea."

"What's a good idea, Mom?"

"Why going to buy your riding outfit for the show. We seem to have a free afternoon ahead of us and there's no time like right now to do it." So Mom headed the car toward the business section of town instead of toward home. "I have a small problem I'm trying to work on myself," she said after driving a couple of minutes in silence. "And a shopping trip will help us both get our problems off our minds long enough for them to stew around and maybe seem a bit easier to solve later on."

Mom maneuvered the car around a slow-moving milk truck. "Did you say you were going to have to jump over something in class, Boo? I didn't know you were ready for that. Maybe Mr. Sikes said something that sounded like jumps. Now what could that be—" And she was off, making harmless conversation just the way I had when she picked me up earlier.

*   *   *

Boy! Riding clothes are expensive! Have you ever checked them out? Well I did. There I was, stuffed into a small, curtained dressing room at the Bit and Bridle Riding Shop trying on breeches and coats and special shirts and vests and other assorted pieces of riding gear. And all the time I was trying them on, my guilt feelings were mounting. I couldn't believe those price tags. Who the heck made the things? The Queen's royal tailors? As far as I was concerned my riding career was still going to come to a screeching halt the day after the horse show. I hadn't changed my mind about being involved with horses. I just wanted to be involved with people, and once summer was over and school had started, horses weren't supposed to be a part of the picture any more. So what was I doing here, spending a small fortune of Mom's money for an outfit I was only going to wear once? Especially when I considered that probably the money that was going to pay for the riding clothes was coming out of the money for this year's school clothes. I was looking more and more unhappy as I kept trying on different things. And Mom and the saleslady were taking my looks in altogether a different way. The saleslady kept saying things like, "But that coat looks lovely on you, dear. The color is so becoming and it fits perfectly. Why, we won't even have to alter it one little bit."

That's great, I thought. Maybe we can return it if I'm careful and don't fall off. Then Mom would agree with the saleslady. And I'd ask if I could try on another one while wondering if there were some way that I could stall Mom on this buying spree until I could talk to her alone.

But there wasn't any. That saleslady was clinging like a couple of wool socks just out of the dryer. I'd tried on everything in my size, and the saleslady's

attitude was getting a little frayed. I looked at Mom and noticed she was beginning to get that tight look between the eyes that means she is about to explode in public and make one of her more artistic scenes. So I grabbed up the jacket that was on the top of the heap and said, "I like this one."

By that time I'd changed back into my horse-smelling jeans, the expensive new clothes were carefully tissued and boxed in tan cardboard with little gold branding irons all over the cardboard. And Mom was writing out a check for the amount.

Mom put the key in the ignition and started the engine, but she didn't put the car in gear. Instead she sat there staring ahead. Sometimes writing checks for large amounts affects her that way, so I didn't say anything, just waited.

"Maybe we shouldn't have gotten you the riding clothes just now. Maybe I should have talked to you first." (Oh, boy! Sometimes I think our mental communication is good . . . and then at other times . . . !) "But you've seemed to be so happy this summer that I was sure this was what you wanted. However, after seeing you in the store just now and seeing how glum you were when I picked you up, I'm not so sure about anything."

Then she started the car. "Tell you what. Why don't we go and have some Chinese?"

Now there are two reasons for Mom to suggest we go and have some Chinese food. One is that there is something to celebrate. (This wasn't one of those times.) The other is when something serious is about to happen and Mom wants to discuss it. (I had a feeling this was one of those times.)

We were the only customers in the Golden Pagoda. It was past the lunch hour and a little too early for dinner. The hostess showed us to a corner booth, and we ordered the #3 combination special. The first course was won ton soup. I finished mine and started munching from a bowl of fried noodles that was sitting in the middle of the table. I noticed that Mom was playing with a piece of seaweed on the bottom of her soup bowl, sort of pushing it into a circle around a mushy bit of won ton. I wondered when she was going to get to whatever it was she wanted to talk about.

Suddenly I had a sticky feeling it was going to be about something I didn't want to hear. Because usually she has launched into whatever it is by this time. I thought back to earlier this afternoon and realized she'd been awfully quick to suggest that buying spree . . . something I usually have to instigate. All at once I didn't want to know. I wondered if maybe I was to explain why I'd been so glum and ask her opinion about my problem, maybe, just maybe, it would change matters enough so that her problem wouldn't be so sticky. So I started telling her all about Troy and Tamara.

Four fried shrimp, two helpings of fried rice, and half an egg roll later I'd pretty much laid things out. I don't know what I'd expected . . . a flash of lightning and instant wisdom, perhaps. Instead, Mom poked at her Moo Goo Guy Pan, ate a mouthful, and then smeared some hot mustard on the edge of her egg roll.

"Well, Boo. As I see it, what you have here is not just one problem. It's two problems, and you need two answers. And the answer to one problem is not doing anything to answer the other one. And I'm sure that that is not the answer you want to hear. But it's my opinion, and please remember that it is only one opinion and you can take it or leave it."

"Mom. I hate to say this. But you sound as loony as one of the sayings inside these fortune cookies. I do not understand one word of what you are saying."

"All right. Let me explain it another way. What's happened is that you've found out something about the two people whom you consider to be your closest friends. And this something is a problem you feel is your duty to solve. Because if you don't, one of them, or possibly both of them, is going to get hurt. But you can't figure how to straighten things out without having to hurt one of them. So, to you, it's a matter of which one to hurt. Right? And you don't want to hurt either of them. But you'll feel guilty if you just let things develop on their own. Right? So I think that you have two problems . . . *how* can you solve their problem, and *should* you? Now, does that make it any clearer?"

"Oh, wow! How can you take a simple problem and turn it into such a complicated situation? I only want to help Tamara and Troy."

"Boo. If it is such a simple problem, why don't you have an answer?"

The waiter came and took our plates and asked if we wanted the kumquat ice cream or almond cookies for dessert. We decided on the almond cookies.

"Well, I don't have an answer. Why do you think I asked you?"

"I told you I didn't think you'd like my answer, Boo. But I can't give you the one you obviously want to hear. I can only give you what I honestly feel is the one I would go with. I think it is best to consider what would be least likely to hurt anyone. And, don't forget, that includes you. Just remember, when two people have a problem and a third party interferes, without being asked to interfere, it is sometimes the third party that is hurt most."

Somehow that last part sounded familiar and I had a feeling Mom could be right . . . though I didn't want to admit it just yet. I still wanted to think about it, and I said so.

Mom's answer was that that was what she would expect of me and I should certainly give it a lot of thought and not just take the first person's advice, no matter who gave it. She said something else about problems not being perfect things and their usually having more than one answer to them. Then she smiled and handed me a fortune cookie and said, "Here. Why don't you let Confucius give you an answer, too."

I half expected to open it and find some saying such as, "A wise man knows when not to speak." But instead mine said, "The bark of a tree is different from that of a dog." Try and come up with some deep philosophical meaning out of that. I showed it to Mom and she cracked up and then showed me hers. It said, "A white cat in the dark is sometimes a black one." It sounded as though the person who wrote the fortunes lived at the SPCA.

Mom picked up the teapot and shook it. There was a little left and she divided it equally between our cups. She sipped at hers and stared at the slip of paper with her fortune on it. Then she rolled it up into a tiny ball and dropped it onto the plate. "It's silly, I know, but I always think that I'll find the answer to whatever problem I'm working on in one of these cookies."

Then I realized that we'd spent the entire meal talking about my problem and we never had gotten around to what it was that Mom wanted to talk to me about. So I asked her.

"Hey, Mom. What was it that you wanted to talk to me about? Was it just because I was being glum?"

"No. Besides, you've answered that for me. I can see now that you have made friends, and good ones. I wasn't sure whether or not you had up until now. But I think you've helped me to solve my problem by telling me yours."

"There you go again, being all mysterious. What is it, Mom? What did you want to talk to me about?"

"Well, I got a letter yesterday from the owner of the house we're living in. It seems that he's going to be staying overseas permanently." She paused and looked at me. "And he's been offered a good deal by someone who would like to buy the house. However, he does realize that he did agree to lease it to us for a year and he needs my permission to sell it. And that, Boo, is my problem."

"I see," was all I could think of to say. And I wondered if this problem had more than one answer. I didn't think so.

10

I'd love to say that both my problems, the one with Tamara and Troy and the bombshell that Mom unloaded, worked themselves out immediately and all was smooth sailing.

But the fact was that Tamara and Troy went right on as usual and I decided not to say anything to either one of them just yet. I was going to let the situation ride, at least until after the show was over. For one reason, I wasn't so sure but that Mom was right when she told me to cool it and keep my nose out of the affair and let them work it out on their own. And the second reason was that Tamara and Troy, along with Sally and the two Weiner brothers, were the best riders Greenway had and I sure as heck wasn't going to be responsible for blowing the show for everybody by getting them all upset.

As for asking Mom if she had made any decision about the house yet, I couldn't seem to make myself do it. It was like when I have a really bad cut or sore, the kind that makes me feel squeamy when I look at it, with blood and goo oozing out and everything. Once the band-aid is on I have no intention of even taking a peek to see how it's coming along. Well, that was how I felt about this. I was hoping if I left the situation alone, it would get well on its own.

But inside I had a sinking feeling that the only possible answer that was right for Mom to make was to tell the owner she would move and that he was free to sell the house. Let me tell you, I was sick about it!

So instead of doing anything about either problem I threw myself into the preparations for the show with almost as much fervor as the others.

I learned, much to the distress of the ever-present yellow streak along my backbone, that I was indeed going to have to take Graham Cracker over two jumps in the Hunter Hack Class. But much to the relief of that same streak, the jumps were only one-and-a-half feet high. However, a jump one-and-a-half feet high looks a lot different from the back of the horse than it does from the ground. And not the way you would expect. It takes on all the aspects of an eight-foot-high, solid brick wall. I think the horse sees it the same way. Anyway, Cracker certainly did. He took no chances and every time we went over it he cleared the jump by about four feet . . . or at least it felt that way.

Sally said that I was lucky because Cracker was a born jumper and rarely ever refused to jump, or tried to go around one. Frankly I think I would have preferred a horse that had the good sense to go around the jump. But that, according to horsedom, isn't playing the game right.

Up until the jumping started I had the impression that I'd turned into at least a passable rider, and I'd gone along with just about everything Mr. Sikes had asked me to do all summer. But this entire jumping thing had definitely taken me my surprise. And I remembered, all too clearly, the discussion I'd had with Deborah that first day about the questionable sanity of anyone who intentionally rode a horse over a jump. Yet here I was, trapped, and all during class I could see her sitting up in the stands, sneering. Righteous little beast! Oh, she'd warned me all right. But I hadn't had the good sense to heed that warning. No, I'd wanted friends . . . and it now appeared it was to be at the cost of my life. Oh, maybe I'm exaggerating just a little. But at one point it seemed the only thing I was capable of doing was riding up to the jump, falling off, and watching as Cracker galloped on down the ring by himself. By the end of the week, though, I had stopped falling off and Mr. Sikes said I actually looked like I knew what I was doing a good percentage of the time.

That was the afternoon we decided (well, actually I had no voice in the matter—I just nodded when they looked in my direction) to form a spy mission to Shadow Hills.

We were sitting under the trees and consuming large quantities of egg salad sandwiches, dill pickles, and grape punch when Grant Hillard said, "What we ought to do is sneak over to the enemy camp and see how our competition is doing." He said this with a perfectly straight face but everyone knew he was joking. That's because Grant Hillard is probably the least likely person to ever perpetrate anything exciting. His idea of daring is to eat two dill pickles at one sitting. Most of us laughed politely. We all like Grant and we pretend to think that he is mildly humorous just to make him happy. But Tamara and Sally weren't laughing. They were looking at each other as if he'd just come up with an idea worthy of the Pentagon.

"Hey," they said in unison. "That's not a bad idea!"

"What's not a bad idea?" said Troy.

"Going over to Shadow Hills," said Sally. "That's a terrific idea!"

"You're out of your tree," said Troy. "You can't do that."

"Why not?" asked Tamara, looking at Troy as if he was the one who was out of his head.

"Because you just can't," said Troy. And it looked like it was starting to turn into a staring match.

"Well, for one reason," said Dennis Weiner, "you can't get into Shadow Hills unless you're a member.

There's a guard at the gate. Secondly, even if you did, when they see you they sure aren't going to trot out their best riders for you to look at."

Tamara wasn't giving up easily. "We're not talking about walking in the front gate, you ninny. We could sneak in through the cross-country jump course at the back of the club and then hide under the grandstand. There's all that lattice-work around the bottom so we could just sit underneath and watch them practice for as long as we wanted and they'd never see us."

Troy wasn't giving in very easily, either. "Tamara, your mind has completely disintegrated. You've been reading too many Nancy Drew books."

You could see the sparks building up in back of Tamara's eyes. But before she could come out with her next statement, Bob Weiner, who's older and who a lot of people consider to be a pretty good judge of what's what, said something that made everybody think. "What happens if, just by chance, you get caught? It might be considered trespassing, you know. And there could be quite a flap if it came to the attention of the show committee. Sure, I know it's not that big a deal. But you know how stuffy and uptight the committee is when it comes to tradition and doing things in a sportsmanlike way. I think you ought to consider that. It's probably what Troy had in mind. You just didn't let him finish what he was going to say, Tamara." (Boy, do guys ever stick together.)

"Thanks, Bob," said Troy in a voice that could have cut steel. "Personally, sure I'd like to see what the competition is that I'm going to be riding against this year. But I don't think it's worth taking the risk. What if the show committee decided to cancel the show? How would you feel?"

"Oh, come on!" Sally said. "Do you really think they would? Just over a little thing like that?"

"They might." Troy looked thoughtful. "When it comes down to the bottom line, the committee would probably consider that tradition and honesty should be upheld, even at the cost of canceling the show. But even if they didn't, they'd make a big stink about it. And how would you feel facing Mr. Sikes? I'm not sure I'd want him to think of me as being unsportsmanlike and dishonest."

"Oh, barf!" sputtered Tamara. "I think you're both being a couple of super-chickens. No one is going to get caught. And you're making too big a deal out of it. If you guys don't want to go—don't go! But Sally and Boo and I are going, aren't we?" And that's when she looked at me and I nodded . . . don't ask me why . . . not everything we do in this life makes sense. "And, of course, Grant, because it was his idea in the first place. Right Grant?" And she succeeded in roping in poor Grant as well.

After that, people took sides. The final group going included Tamara, Sally, Grant, Dennis, and me. Troy and Bob declined . . . and not at all gracefully. In fact, they showed their disgust with the entire idea pretty strongly and left, muttering something about us ruining the reputation of Greenway.

I could see Tamara was absolutely burning because Troy hadn't gone along with her plan. But born leader that she was, she wasn't letting a minor thing like a little dissent among the troops upset the planning of her maneuvers. We refilled our cups with grape punch and sat around the table while she sketched the layout of the Shadow Hills Club. By the time the session was over we had been well briefed and knew the roles we were to play.

11

Frankly I was beginning to feel that Troy had been one-hundred-percent correct in his evaluation of Tamara and this stupid mission.

If you're ever looking for a really terrific, fun place to spend a blistering hot August day, don't make it the underside of a splintery old grandstand. And let me say this, that for a super-posh riding club, their under-grandstand housekeeping left much to be desired. There were popcorn bags, hot dog wrappers, and soft drink bottles dating from the year one, all piled so deep that if anyone dropped a lighted match down into that mess we'd all go off like Roman candles. And the pervading smell, which grew steadily stronger as the day grew hotter, was one of an indescribable origin, with overtones of dead things and sneakers that haven't been washed since the beginning of summer.

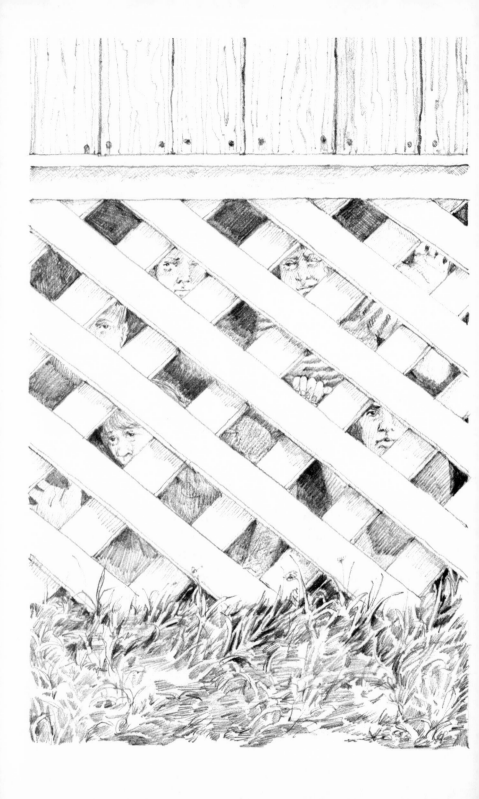

As for the success of the mission: Yes, we'd made it to the grandstand and we'd been able to find a broken place at the back of the stand so we could crawl through and hide underneath. But just in case you're wondering, and I can't imagine why you would, there isn't a lot you can see between the slats of lattice-work around the bottom of a grandstand.

We were scrunched in a kind of human pretzel fashion about as close to the front as we could get. If you put your head at a comfortable level all you could see were a lot of hoofs doing something, but you couldn't tell what. If you turned your head at a right angle to your body and put your eye to the space between the wood slats you could see what the horses were doing at the far end of the ring and some-times in part of the center. But the thing that they were doing at the far end of the ring, and in the cen-ter, would also bring them galloping past our hiding place. So that, since there were only about two or three feet between where the horses passed and where we were scrunched, whatever eye was being held next to the opening would receive a large helping of dust and dried horse manure. It was enough to discourage even the most gung-ho spy.

All of us, with the exception of Tamara, had given up. I was beginning to suspect that she was only try-ing to show us that she still felt the mission was a suc-cess. I looked at her. She must have been feeling pretty low and I had to admire her for keeping up a front. I don't think I could have. But I guess that's what makes a leader. And I was sure that those leadership qualities would help her to rise to fight again.

But the way I was feeling was that I sure as heck was never going to rise again. My neck appeared to be stuck permanently at a sixty-degree angle from my body. And my left leg had definitely become disassociated from the rest of me as there hadn't been any feeling in it for at least half an hour.

I looked at the others. Sally was showing her hostility to the situation by sketching things like daggers and guns in the dirt with an old popsicle stick. Dennis had completely given up. Choosing comfort over anything remotely resembling cleanliness, he was lying prone among the debris. As for Grant, he'd put a sort of simpy smile on his face whenever you'd look in his direction. But you could tell he definitely wasn't happy and the smile was a phony. Poor Grant. He is one of those insecure guys who feels he always has to be nice, no matter what, because he wants to be liked and thinks that is the way to do it. If only he would break loose once in a while and let his feelings show. It would probably not be such a strain on everyone and we'd all like him a heck of a lot more.

But as far as anyone expressing feelings vocally at the moment, it wasn't possible. Not unless we wanted to be discovered almost instantly because there were people sitting on top of us. Oh, you know what I mean. The grandstand seats were between us and them so we weren't being crushed, or anything, but they were sitting right over our heads. And if anybody as much as whispered something like, "I've got to go to the bathroom," which I did indeed need to do . . . why we'd be discovered for sure.

We'd been under there at least three hours, maybe four, and there hadn't been any sign that the people in the grandstand, or the horses in the ring, were going to go elsewhere.

I tapped Tamara on the shoulder. She turned around and looked out at me through dirt-ringed eyes that made her look like a raccoon. I mouthed, "When are we going to leave?"

"When they leave," she mouthed back. And she pointed upward with one hand and in the direction of the ring with the other.

"How much longer before they leave?" I mouthed. (Who knows why you ask a stupid question like that. As if Tamara knew anymore about it than I did.)

"How should I know?" she mouthed. And she looked at me as if I'd just asked a really stupid question. (Which I have just admitted was true.)

"Well, I hope it's soon," I almost said out loud. And I made a face that showed her I wasn't at all happy with the situation.

"Sorry!" she almost hissed. And it wasn't the kind of sorry that really meant sorry. Then she shrugged her shoulders, or at least made an attempt, because we were already so scrunched up that the only way you could shrug your shoulders would be downward, and that's silly.

She turned around and went back to peering out through the slats.

I sat peeling my fingernails and thinking about the same old question that I always ask myself in situations like this. Would I rather be dying of thirst or in need of finding a restroom? My answer is always the same. Dying of thirst is much better.

Desperation sometimes gives rise to acts of courage and daring. And I can't, offhand, think of any situation that involves more desperation than having to go to the bathroom and not having a bathroom handy.

So ignoring any possible further confrontation with Tamara on the subject of leaving, I looked at Sally and Grant and put my finger to my mouth in a shush sign. Then I crawled toward where we'd come in, at the back of the stand. I peered out and there wasn't a living thing out there, with the exception of two squirrels who were arguing over a peanut butter sandwich. At a distance, to my left, I could see a dark green building with entrances on either side. I looked longingly at it. But I knew if I went in that direction, and even if I made it to the building without being seen, it was ten to one that some girl club member was going to be in there brushing her hair or slopping on mascara or something. Ahead of me was the open cross-country jump course, and it was definitely open territory. But to my right was a thick clump of trees that backed up to the restaurant part of the club. I have enough camping experience in back of me so that I know what to do with a clump of trees. I crawled out of the hole and headed for them.

Afterward I wondered if I was going to make it back to the stand as easily as I made it to the trees. Then I thought how really stupid it would be to go back there. I have never considered myself to be a masochist, and standing up straight and breathing fresh air was very nice for a change. I thought about staying hidden in the trees until the others decided to leave and I sat down behind a clumpy bush that hid me pretty well and waited.

I didn't have to wait long. Almost immediately Sally looked out, looked right and left, and came running toward my clump in a bent-over, zigzag manner, looking very much like a spy in one of those corny movies. Which, come to think of it, just about summed up what we were . . . some corny kind of spies. Grant followed almost immediately after Sally. He didn't zigzag, he scuttled—also looking like a silly spy. There was a hesitation and then Dennis crawled out, stood up, and started to saunter in our direction. I guess he figured if no one had made a fuss so far, he was safe. But about a third of the way across he suddenly broke into a run and ended up with a clunk beside the rest of us.

The bush had been more than ample when it had been used to hide just me. Even after Sally came it had still been successful. But as Grant had joined us it had seemingly started to shrivel. And by the time Dennis, who is very tall for his age, clunked in beside us, the bush had shrunk to fig leaf size. And there we were —a lot of arms and legs sticking out in all directions from a round green ball.

Dennis sized up the situation in a hurry. "Well, we can't stay here too long. Someone will see us."

"What about Tamara?" Sally was a stickler for leaving anywhere with the same number of people that she'd come with.

"Does she realize that we've left?" Grant asked Dennis.

"Hmm! I don't know. Come to think of it she was still looking out at the ring when I left. Do you suppose she didn't hear us go?" I don't know who he expected to answer that.

Then I said what I think we were all beginning to wonder. "Do you think someone should go back and get her? I mean, we can't just leave her there."

In the minute or so that followed you never heard so much silence as there was behind that bush.

"OK, OK. I'll go." I said. It seemed that I had taken temporary leadership because I had been the one to start the exodus. (I wonder if anyone else has ever assumed leadership because of the need to go to the bathroom.) So I left the security of my bush and ran back to the grandstand. I stuck my head in the hole and threw an empty aluminum soft drink can in the direction of Tamara's back to get her attention. When she turned around I motioned to her in a way that pretty clearly meant—"Let's get the heck out of here."

A wise leader knows when to retreat . . . and I've always said Tamara was a wise leader.

So we got out. And we got away from the club grounds. And nothing disastrous happened . . . not even a raised eyebrow from one of the squirrels. But we did get some rather peculiar looks from the bus driver when we boarded the bus back for the other side of town. And some of the passengers did get up and move to another section of the bus.

But that was about it for our mission.

*   *   *

As for the problem between Tamara and Troy, maybe Mom had been right in suggesting it would work itself out. (Although I don't see how she could possibly have known in advance about the mission to Shadow Hills, or how it would turn out. Or how the outcome would affect Tamara's feelings toward Troy.) Because later on that evening Tamara confided to me that she couldn't understand how she'd ever considered Troy as boyfriend material . . . distant friend, yes . . . boyfriend, no! Isn't it strange how a leader will react to defeat. Troy's decision to have absolutely no part of our plan hadn't bothered her all that much. Probably because they were always disagreeing with each other over something. But I guess this had been the first time that she'd ever been proven so enormously wrong, and in front of so many people. Oh, she'd admitted that defeat, but she still had to save face. Even if it was only to herself and, maybe, to her best friend. I think she knew that I knew that this was what she was doing and it wasn't going to go any farther. But I was pretty sure too that the boy-girl relationship was over and the just-plain-good-friend relationship would get back to where it belonged.

12

I'm not sure who it is that decides these things . . . nature, fate, or whoever. But there seems to be some kind of a law that if you get one problem solved, another is going to pop up and take its place. Not always right away, but soon enough so that you know the problem you're getting is replacing the one that just got solved.

And that's the way it was this time.

After Tamara had told me about how she felt regarding Troy as a boyfriend, I'd gone to bed feeling as though someone had taken the whole thing off my hands. I was darned grateful and said so into the darkness of my room.

And even though Tamara and Troy weren't speaking, I figured it was only a matter of time before they'd get around to it. And I was right. But it took the latest in the series of Boo's personal problems to do it.

This particular problem began on the day before the show. We'd just finished having a last class in which we'd run through what we were going to be doing in the show. We were all feeling pretty good about how well we'd done and being lazy, sitting on our horses in the middle of the ring and not paying much attention to what they were doing. (You are never supposed to do that, but when the sun is warm and you feel pretty good it sometimes happens.)

Graham Cracker and I were next to Tamara and her horse, Sun's Up. Tamara and I were laughing about something that Grant had done in class and Cracker and Sun's Up must have started a conversation, too. But it wasn't a friendly one. Because both of them put their ears back and before you could say whoa, there were hoofs and teeth flying every which way and Tamara and I had our hands full of reins and manes, and anything else we could get hold of, trying to get Cracker and Sun's Up away from each other.

It didn't last long. But that's relative. Because it was long enough so that both Cracker and Sun's Up came out of the fight bleeding. Mr. Sikes ran over and looked at both of them and said he didn't think that either of them was too badly hurt as the cuts were superficial, but that he'd better go and call Dr. Simpkin (that's the veterinarian who takes care of the Greenway horses) and have him come out and take a look at them anyway.

I glanced over to where Tamara was standing with Sun's Up and noticed that Troy had forgotten all about his differences and had gone right over to help her as she seemed a bit shaky about the whole thing. She seemed glad to have him help her.

Then I realized that I was pretty shaken up myself. Sally came over and helped me get the saddle and bridle off Cracker and put a halter on him. As I was taking the saddle off I noticed a place on Cracker's shoulder that was beginning to swell, and he didn't seem to want to put his weight on that leg. I called to Mr. Sikes and he came over and felt the bulge. Then he sighed and massaged his chin for a moment and looked thoughtful. He told Sally to go and get the hose and see if it would stretch far enough to reach where we were standing and, if it would, to start running cold water over the shoulder. But if it didn't, to get a bucket of water and start squeezing water over the bump with a sponge.

Sally ran to hook up the hose. And it reached, just barely. She put the cold stream of water on his shoulder. Cracker flinched just a little and then stood there very patiently, but still not putting his foot on the ground. I stood by his head and held the lead while I stroked his neck and told him how much I loved him and that everything was going to be OK when Dr. Simpkin got there . . . you know . . . saying the kind of thing you automatically say to an animal that's nervous and hurt . . . and I guess, to help calm yourself down as well.

But after the first few minutes of talking to him I suddenly realized that I was crying and that I meant every word of what I was saying to him. I did love him—the silly little beast.

And now he was hurt. And it was because I'd been stupid and careless.

I don't know how long we stood there. But long enough so that Mr. Sikes came over twice to feel Cracker's shoulder and smile at me and try to reassure me. But each time he did I could see his face crumple from a smiling one to a worried one as soon as he'd turned away.

Finally Dr. Simpkin's white pick-up truck, with all the special boxes built into the back so that it acted as a sort of rolling hospital, came bouncing over the dirt road; fast enough so that it raised a large mushroom dust cloud that sailed off toward the sky.

Dr. Simpkin got out of his truck and stood talking with Mr. Sikes for a minute and then they came walking toward us, their heads together with Mr. Sikes gesturing with both hands, probably describing what had happened. When they'd reached us Mr. Sikes took the lead out of my hand, put his hand lightly on my shoulder, and then told us to go and sit on the bench near the barn so we wouldn't be in Dr. Simpkin's way.

I sat and watched Dr. Simpkin poke at Cracker's shoulder and make him take a step that he didn't want to take. As I sat there, I remembered that time earlier in the summer when Wentworth had disappeared the day after we'd moved into our new house and Jonathan had sat on the stairs looking so totally lost. Well, sitting there on the bench, that was just the way I felt.

As I thought about it I couldn't really figure out why I was feeling that way. Why, Cracker didn't even belong to me. He was just a dumb old pony that Mr. Sikes used to teach kids to ride. And I didn't even like horses!

But I'd just told Cracker I loved him and I guessed that meant I did . . . like horses, I mean.

It shook me up so much that I stopped sniffing and made a funny, half-laugh "huh" sound to myself.

Sally must have misunderstood my "huh" sound because she reached over and patted my knee and said, "Don't worry. Cracker's going to be OK, I'm sure. And Mr. Sikes doesn't blame you. Those things happen. It's probably nothing but a bad bump. You know, like the kind you get when you fall off."

I looked at her, not even caring if she could see the tear tracks down my cheek—it was that terrible, the way I felt. "Do you really think it's not bad?" I said. "I mean his shoulder isn't broken, or anything, so they're going to have to shoot him?"

Then Sally let out a "huh" sound. But this "huh" sound was more like a cross between "how stupid can you be" and "oh you poor kid." "No!" she said out loud. "Whatever it is, it isn't that bad. But what's really bad is that you might not be able to ride Cracker in the show tomorrow. Because a bump like that could very well lay him up for a week, or a month, or a couple of months. That's what you've got to worry about."

At that a whole bunch of mixed emotions fell into my thinking pattern. I was glad Cracker's shoulder probably wasn't going to be all that serious. But what Sally said about not being in the show . . . that was another thing. In the beginning I'd hated the idea. I would have done almost anything to have gotten out of being in it. Then I'd become used to the idea and accepted it as one of those things you have to do. And it had been my personal opinion that that was about where my true feelings stood on the matter.

But now . . . now that I had an out . . . I didn't want it! The idea that there was now about a million-to-one chance (there's that million again but this time it's about right) that I was very likely not going to ride in the show started a very cold knot growing in my stomach. And it grew and grew and grew until I felt cold all over. Not being able to ride in the show turned into a very horrible thing indeed. I thought about all the times I'd fallen off Cracker when I'd tried to learn how to jump and how Mr. Sikes had told me that I was looking pretty good and I might even place in my classes and about my new riding clothes hanging up on the door of my closet at home and about a lot of other things, so that I didn't even notice when

Dr. Simpkin left and Mr. Sikes came over and took Sally's place and sat down beside me.

Sally had been right on all counts. Cracker's bump was just that, a very bad bump. And he would be OK. But he wouldn't be OK in time for the show. It was Dr. Simpkin's opinion that he should rest up and not be ridden for at least a week and then not before he gave his OK. And Sun's Up was lucky because all he had was just a superficial cut that a band-aid would have taken care of—if horses could wear band-aids. So Tamara would be able to ride him in the show. And that was lucky for all of us because we needed her to ride for the club.

Then he said something that surprised me. He told me that the club needed me to ride in the show, too. He wasn't sure just how he was going to work it but to give him a little while and he would come up with something.

Then he said that while he was doing his cogitating why didn't I help Sally get Rally Round ready.

For you who've never gotten a horse ready for a show, let me tell you that you spend just about ten times as much time getting that horse ready as you do riding in the show itself.

First of all, you have to groom that horse until he's so shiny that you can practically see yourself looking back at yourself when you look at his coat. And if he's white, or some light color, you probably have to give him a bath, too. Sally's horse, Rally Round, was light gray with dark spots so he didn't need a complete bath, but he did need a bit of organized scrubbing here and there. He liked to roll a lot and had grass stains on his knees and some on his hocks. And grass stains are just as hard to get off a horse as they are to get off clothes. Furthermore, you can't just throw a horse into a washing machine.

Then, after the horse is all clean, and if you are going to ride him English—which is about the only kind of riding you do in Virginia—you have to braid his mane and tail. There's an awful lot of mane and tail to a horse. They have to be done up in these super-tight little braids that have to be sewn together with carpet thread so that they won't come out when you're riding fast around the ring, or going over a jump. It takes a lot of time to do them right. And if they aren't done right, Mr. Sikes makes you take them out and do them all over again until they are right.

Even then you aren't through. Because there's the saddle and bridle, and anything else that is going to go on the horse, that has to be cleaned and polished until it shines as well.

Mr. Sikes is not one to let things go until the day of the show. He checks and double checks everything and nobody goes home until everything is ready.

I was busy helping Sally. We'd finished scrubbing off the grass stains as well as we could and they were about dry enough so that she was starting to work some chalk dust into them. That way they wouldn't look so greenish-yellow.

I had heard a horse neigh and looked up to see Mr. Sikes leading one toward us. At first I thought it was his horse, Jeep. But as he came closer I noticed that it wasn't. Jeep wasn't that big!

"Boo, this is Blunderbuss. He is not exactly the horse I would prefer you to be mounted on for the show, but he is as close as we're going to get to a good mount you can handle in the short time we have. He belongs to a very old friend of mine who is retired. And, in fact, you might say Blunderbuss is sort of retired as well. He's old but he's reliable and I think the two of you will get on just fine."

I looked at Blunderbuss and knew that this had to be the classic case of not suiting the rider to the horse and the horse to the rider. Because Blunderbuss was just about the tallest horse I'd ever seen in my entire life. I was going to need a ladder just to reach his knee.

"Come on, Boo," said Mr. Sikes. "Let's go over to the ring and see how you do on him."

So I gave the can of chalk dust I was holding to Sally and followed Mr. Sikes and Blunderbuss over to the ring; all the while wondering what the world was going to look like mounted on an animal the size of some prehistoric monster.

It wasn't long before I found out. Tiny is the word. From up there, everything looked tiny. And it had me a little scared. No! Scared is not the word. It seemed that my newly found love of horses had a height factor involved. Terrified is the word. I was terrified out of my mind.

But I wasn't going to let Mr. Sikes know.

13

I'm not sure how much pressure the human body and mind will take before it goes sprong! But I'm sure that mine had just about reached the maximum.

I looked around me at the others waiting to ride in the gate of the Shadow Hills ring. Class number six, "Beginner's Equitation for Riders under Twelve," was just finishing up. If you count right, that meant that class number seven, "Beginner's Equitation for Riders Thirteen and Over," was up next. And that was me.

I am not supersitious or anything like that, you understand, but I had been glad when I'd heard my class number was seven. However, as I counted the kids grouped about me, including myself, the number came to thirteen. Well, so much for luck! It looked like I'd better count more on what I could remember from my summer's worth of lessons. However, due to a numbness of mind and a totally disassociated feeling of various legs and arms which were supposedly mine, that didn't seem like it was going to be very much.

From someplace in another world I heard a lot of clapping and yelling, showing that class number six was over. Kids came dribbling out through the gate. Some had happy looks and assorted colored ribbons clenched in their hands, or between their teeth if their hands were too full of reins. Others with set expressions looked ahead of them, or down, hiding what kind of feelings I wondered. Then they were past us and it was our turn.

I gathered up the reins, patted Blunderbuss on the neck, wished to all the gods that might be listening it was Cracker I was riding instead of him, and trotted into the ring feeling like King Kong on top of the Empire State Building. Only my building was alive and moving.

I think that class gave me a little bit better understanding of the relativity of time. Because, on one hand, the class seemed to go on and on and on forever, like one of those pieces of action film they slow down so that everyone looks like they're moving under about twenty tons of water. Yet, on the other hand, it seemed as if the class couldn't have lasted over thirty or forty seconds.

I was aware of doing everything the judge asked us to, like trotting and cantering and reversing the way we were going and finally lining up in the center of the ring and then backing individually as the judge walked down the line of horses facing him. And yet, I don't remember doing it . . . not actually. It was more like I'd been programmed and the tape had run through all on its own, without my interference.

I haven't the slightest idea as to what kind of expression was on my face as class number seven left the ring, riding past class number eight, all grouped and ready to go in after us. Nor do I remember hearing any clapping or yelling, but there must have been. Can people function like that? Boy, I don't want to have to do it too often.

"A second! Oh, Boo! That's terrific!" Tamara grabbed the ribbon out of my hand and held it up.

"Great!" said Troy. "That's six more points for our side." And he took the ribbon from Tamara and pinned it up on the board holding all the others that had been won by our team so far.

"Fantastic, Boo!" said Sally. And she gave me a little hug.

"Here comes Grant," said Dennis. "He's got a fourth. That's another point for us."

Bob Weiner took the ribbon from Grant and gravely shook his hand, then pinned the ribbon on the board under mine.

"That's all very nice. But you're still way behind. And there's no way you're going to catch up." Deborah, the little pill, was sitting on a rolled-up

sleeping bag, munching on a candied apple and looking superior.

"Who's side are you on, anyway, Deborah?"
glowered Troy.

"I'm on your side, naturally," said Deborah. "But I
still believe in telling it like it is. And like it is, is that
you're losing. Sorry!" And she threw the remains of
the apple and stick toward a trash can about ten feet
away. The apple went splat and slid down the side of
the can.

"Go pick that up and put it where it belongs," said
Troy. "And then put yourself in with it."

"You don't tell me what to do," said Deborah, "and
I won't tell you what to do, brother dear." But she
went and picked up the apple anyway, deposited it,
and then stalked off. No doubt to get another one.

"You know she's right," said Dennis. "The competition really is tough this year. Even worse than the last
couple of years. Have you looked at some of the
Shadow Hill riders working out in the exercise ring?
Man, they've got jumpers that are going to walk all
over ours."

"I know, I know!" said Troy. "But listen, I've been
watching, too. And what's really going to make it are
the novice and green hunter classes coming up this
afternoon. They've got only a couple of top riders for
those classes and Tamara and Sally are just as good as
they are. If they can only get the breaks and have
clean rounds, without knocking down any of the
jumps, we just might be able to pull this show off."

"If, if . . . you're as bad as your sister," said Dennis. "Only the other way around." And he hit the doorjamb of the stall with his crop. "Just what's to keep their riders from making clean rounds as well? Let's face it. We're never going to win one of these shows. Shadow Hill has the money and the horses and the trainers and everything else it takes. I don't care what kind of point system they use. We just don't have a chance."

"Well, I for one don't want to talk about it any longer," said Tamara. "It would be nice if someone came along and performed a small miracle, like turning their riders into stone for the afternoon, but I seriously doubt that's going to happen. And I'm not going to worry about it any longer."

"Well, maybe you should worry about it just a little," said Troy.

"Well, maybe you could bribe Deborah to poison their horses. All she'd have to do is look at them."

"I don't think that was called for, Tamara!" said Troy. And it looked as though Tamara and Troy were back to business as usual.

"Oh, forget it, Troy. I'm sorry. I'm just nervous, that's all. Come on. Let's all go get a hot dog. Coming, Boo?"

Everybody had stood up and was getting ready to go, but I was still kind of in a daze about having won anything at a horse show, let alone second place.

"Uhm! I think I'd better go over and say hi to my mom and my brother. I haven't talked to them since they got here." Then, although I felt stupid about the next thing that I asked, it came out anyway. "Do you think it would be OK to take my ribbon over and show it to them? Uh, I don't think they've ever seen a horse show ribbon before." Oh, boy! Oh, boy! I knew I was about to go sprong. What a dumb thing to say.

"Oh, heck, yeh!" said Tamara. "Go ahead. We understand. See ya after lunch." And she bounced over next to Troy, ready to get back into the fray. She looked back long enough to smile and say, "Don't forget to pray for a miracle while you're eating lunch, OK?"

I went over to the board and took my ribbon down, careful not to disturb the ones on either side of it. The show committee sure hadn't stinted on the awards. It was one of those ones that have the pleated rosette around a big gold center and two long satin streamers hanging down. I know it's not really cool to want to go and show a stupid ribbon to your mom when you're my age, and everything. But, for some reason, I didn't care. I really wanted to share this with mom and . . . even Jonathan.

I was glad that I did. I could tell she was as excited as I was and wanted to tell me that. Jonathan was jumping up and down saying something about how he was glad he had a famous sister. I didn't bother to correct him about how winning second place in a horse show class does not exactly make one famous. What the heck!

Nothing was happening in the ring right then, as lunch break had been announced, so Mom suggested that we all go get hot dogs and Cokes and walk around a little. We'd just finished smearing our hot dogs with mustard and catsup from little jars outside the food booth, and I was about to take a large bite when I looked at Jonathan. He'd suddenly turned a funny shade of greenish-white. Mom looked at him too, and said, "Jonathan, what's the matter? Are you sick?"

"Wentworth!" he said.

"Wentworth?" Mom and I both asked together. Not again, I thought.

"He's in my pocket. What if somebody steps on him?"

"What if somebody steps on him?" I said.

"What pocket?" Mom was more to the point.

"The pocket in my jacket," Jonathan said. "I took it off because it got hot. I left it on my seat." He pushed his hot dog in my direction and his coke at Mom. "I'll be right back."

Mom took the Coke. Then she gritted her teeth and through them said, "Jonathan. . . ."

I don't know what else she was about to say, but it wouldn't have mattered because Jonathan was half-way back to the grandstand by that time.

But it wasn't soon enough.

At least not soon enough for the two girls from Shadow Hills who had picked the grandstand as a place to eat their lunch.

As we put it together a little later on, Wentworth must have missed the warmth of Jonathan's body when Jonathan had taken off his jacket, and had decided to go looking for him. What he'd found instead was a hunt cap one of the girls had left nearby. He'd crawled into that and gone to sleep. Then, when the girl had picked up the hat, she hadn't noticed that Wentworth was a temporary resident and had started to put it on her head.

Well you can use your imagination for what happened after that. I don't want to. But it shook the owner of the hat up enough so that she had to lie down with cold compresses on her head. And the friend Wentworth had bounced off of as the hat had gone sailing by wasn't feeling in such great shape either.

The upshot was they both said they didn't think they were up to riding in any of the afternoon classes.

So maybe that was the miracle that Tamara had been looking for. Because, of all the people's hats that Wentworth could have chosen to nap in, he'd picked the best rider that Shadow Hills had. And her friend was the next best rider that Shadow Hills had.

So go ahead and say that those kinds of things happen only in books. Well, let me tell you, they happen in real life, too. I should know.

Jonathan was worried and wanted to form a search party to find Wentworth. But Mom and I both threatened Jonathan that if he let on the snake belonged to him we'd cut off his supply of goat cheese and papayas. The last thing we needed was publicity for Wentworth. We both knew that Wentworth was not the swiftest snake in the east so he still had to be somewhere under that grandstand. It was only a question of sending Jonathan in after him. I even showed him the way in . . . through the same place where we'd gotten in when we'd come on our spy mission.

I left Jonathan crawling about under the grandstand and Mom sitting nervously on top of the grandstand while I went back to get ready for my afternoon class . . . the one in which I was to jump over two jumps while riding on a horse that terrified me because I was already so high off the ground just sitting on him.

As it turned out I needn't have worried about the jumping part at all. Because I found Wentworth first, or rather Blunderbuss did.

At the last moment, while cantering toward the first jump, I decided the best thing to do was to close my eyes and not look again until after we'd gone over it. I shouldn't have done that. Blunderbuss was not Graham Cracker. At the last minute he made a decision, too. His decision was to go around the jump. With my eyes closed I didn't realize this and I was all set to go over it. I did . . . all on my own.

The first thing I saw when I opened my eyes, upon taking flight, was Wentworth . . . hightailing it away

from the jump and back between the slats of the lattice-work at the bottom of the grandstand. The next thing I noticed was a bunch of legs running towards where I lay sprawled in the dirt with guck all over my new riding clothes.

And that was too much. I closed my eyes again.

14

That's about it. That's the end of the story. Though I don't think you could classify it as a very satisfactory ending. Do you?

After I'd been picked up out of the dirt, and in front of all those people, mind you, they'd taken me to an emergency hospital about two miles away from the riding club where a doctor (not even a cute one) had put plaster all over my leg. Then they'd kept me in the emergency room for about four more hours while I watched an assortment of injuries come and go. Finally, they told Mom she could take me home.

Mom fixed the couch up in the living room and that's where I stayed last night. This morning she and Jonathan, together, hauled my poor, broken body out here to the porch for the day.

That was ages ago.

Earlier I'd seen Tamara leave in Dennis and Bob's car and I knew that they, along with the others, were off to spend the day at Chris Green Lake.

Then, at about ten o'clock, Mom had come out to the porch and told me she had to leave for an appointment at the real estate office to talk about the house. I knew what that meant and my misery was only compounded about a thousand times. Because that meant we'd probably have to move before I'd even gotten well enough to go up and see my room for one last time.

Mom had brought out a pitcher of iced tea before she'd left. But it was warm now. I'd used up all the ice cubes to rub around the top of the cast and down my neck to try and cool off. But doing that with the ice made my leg start to itch, and I'd sent Jonathan off to get a wire coat hanger so I could use it to locate the itch and scratch it. But that was a long time ago. I started to yell for him again.

The screen door banged and it was Jonathan. But the only thing I could see that he had with him was Wentworth. Like an overprotective parent, Jonathan hadn't let Wentworth out of his sight since yesterday, when he'd finally retrieved him from under the grandstand. I certainly hoped it would be a phase that didn't have lasting qualities.

"Where's my hanger, Jonathan? Or can't your brain function long enough to retain simple orders?" I said.

"There aren't any wire hangers in the house, Boo. I looked in all the closets. I think Mom threw them all out when she cleaned last week. You know how she hates wire coathangers!"

"Yeh, I know, Jonathan. OK. You did your best and I commend you. Thanks anyway." I knew he was right. Mom has this paranoid thing about wire coathangers. She says they make dents in your clothes, or something.

"But I got you something else that might work." And he held out this long, wicked-looking, plastic thing that was part of his scientific equipment. I took it and said "Thanks," wondered what form of germ warfare was loaded on its surface and decided the best thing would be to let my itch continue to itch.

Jonathan sat down on the steps to be companionable. "Visiting the invalid" is how I think he put it.

He was sitting there drinking some of the lukewarm tea when a car pulled up to the curb. It was Dennis and Bob's. I wondered if Tamara had forgotten something. But then the car doors opened and not only Tamara, but Troy and Bob and Dennis and Sally and Grant, all got out. Bob handed something that looked like a large bowl to Tamara. Tamara and Sally carried it ceremoniously forward to where I was sitting. They were bringing me something. But what?

Do you realize just how embarrassing these kinds of moments are? My first thought was that my hair must be a mess because I hadn't had a chance to wash it since my fall. And even though Mom had helped me put dry shampoo into it and I had brushed it like crazy, it still had a faint aroma of horse. But my second thought was worse yet. Because the realization struck me that there were Tamara and Sally marching straight up the walk toward Jonathan . . . and Wentworth.

"Jonathan!" I hissed. "Get Wentworth into the house . . . now. Please!"

Jonathan (will wonders never cease) actually started to get up and do as I'd asked him. But a yell from someone down on the walk stopped him.

It was Tamara (another wonder). "No, Jonathan, wait. This is for Wentworth, too."

And she and Sally put down the bowl on the top of the steps. But I noticed, for all that Tamara had protested, she was taking no chances and stood as far away from Wentworth as was physically possible.

I looked down at the bowl and noticed it was filled with water, faintly muddy with a piece of pond weed floating on the surface.

"It's for you. Wentworth, too!" Tamara said in the role of spokeswoman. "WE ALMOST WON!" she bounced. "It was all because of you . . . and Wentworth."

"Huh!" (How's that for gracious dialogue?)

Then Troy took over. "Well, actually it was Wentworth. Because the two girls he scared were the riders of the two best horses at Shadow Hills. Without them competing against us, Sally and Tamara won the classes."

"We were only six points behind at the end of the show!" Tamara screamed.

"Oh!" I said. I know I should have said something like "that's great," but somehow what had happened didn't seem quite right.

Dennis must have seen my look for he said, "Before you start thinking that was an unfair advantage on our part, don't! Because even Mr. Sikes agreed that Shadow Hills has had an unfair advantage over us for years. They've been using horses that cost more for one horse than all of the Greenway horses put together. Furthermore, the kids don't even train the horses themselves, professional trainers do it, and I think that's unfair!"

Troy added, "Mr. Sikes is going to talk to the show committee next week and see if we can't make the shows a little more equal from now on."

"We ARE going to WIN next year!" said Tamara sounding like a cheerleader. I could see she already was planning her strategy.

Then Bob explained the contents of the bowl. "We decided that since you can't go to Chris Green Lake with us, we'd bring some of Chris Green Lake to you, so here it is."

"Great!" (There, I said great.)

Then we all looked at each other and I knew they really wanted to get going back to the lake so I said, "Hey! That really is great! About everything, I mean. But why don't you guys get going. Who needs to sit around here if you don't have to."

That broke things up and they smiled and headed back to the car. I waved as they drove off. After they'd gone I realized I had a big fat lump in my throat and my eyes were getting a little foggy. Funny how something as dumb as a bowl of water can make you feel happy.

"What are you crying for, Boo?" said Jonathan. "Does your leg really hurt that much? Can I get you anything else?"

"No. And I'm not crying," I said, sounding kind of muffled because I didn't want him to know I was. "And stop being so blasted nice. I can't stand you that way. I like you better when you're normal. Go play with your encyclopedia or something."

"Oh, OK," he said, and got up to leave.

But as he was about to slam the screen door I said, "Hey, Jonathan! You know you're kind of OK—for a brother, that is."

He looked at me for a second and then said, "You too—for a sister." Then he slammed the door and I was alone.

I sat there for a while, watching the heat waves rising up from the empty asphalt in the street. The mailman came and left, bringing the telephone bill and something labeled Occupant. Mrs. Witherington came out of her house across the street and started puttering in her flower bed. After a while I heard a phone ringing somewhere. Mr. Witherington came to the front door and called for Mrs. Witherington. So I guessed it was for her.

I picked up an issue of *Seventeen* that Mom had left for me and thumbed through it looking at the back-to-school clothes and wondering which of them would look all right with my cast. My leg did hurt a little and I experimented with pouring the last bit of tea down the cast, but I think it only made things worse.

Strange how quiet a neighborhood can be in the middle of a summer day. Pretty soon I guess I fell asleep because when I looked up again, the shadow of the honeysuckle vine had moved over about three feet, and Mom was coming up the front walk. She waved and I saw she had a happy look on her face.

"Hi, Boo. Feeling any better? Here, I brought some ice cream . . . rocky road. Want any?"

"Yeah, I guess so."

"Good. I'll go put some in a dish. Be right back."

In a couple of minutes she handed me a dish and then sat down on the swing and started on the dish she'd brought for herself. At least she started playing with her spoon, pushing the ice cream around. She put the spoon down in the dish and looked at me. "Boo. I've done something and I hope you're going to think it's all right." She paused and picked up the spoon again and looked at it like she'd never seen one before. "It's about the house."

Boy! I knew it! Here it was. I guess the ice cream had been meant to replace a Chinese dinner. "Sure, Mom. I understand! When do we have to move?"

"That's just it, Boo. We don't . . . if you don't want to."

I stared at her. I think my mind was trying to tell me that what she was saying was that we could stay in the house after all. But I didn't want to say it out loud, because I was afraid then Mom would have to say that wasn't what she'd really meant after all. You know, like if I didn't come right out and say it, I could just sit there and think happy thoughts until dooms-day.

Mom saw my look and gave a little laugh. "It's OK, Boo! I really mean it this time." She smiled and I could see she really did. Then she went on, "You know, I think I like it here almost as much as you do. Anyway, I talked to the real estate man and he con-tacted the owner who's perfectly willing to sell the house to us instead of the other person." She paused and put the dish of ice cream down on the floor. "If we want it that is!" She looked at me and I knew it was my turn to talk.

Funny thing, there suddenly seemed to be about a million (there's that million again) things I wanted to say, all at once. But what came out was just . . .

"Fantastic!"

*   *   *

After dinner, that night, Tamara come over. We talked. You know, just talk, nothing earth-shattering or deep. It was comfortable. We sat for a while and watched the fireflies signaling to each other. It got dark and there was some lightning way over in the east, followed by some thunder a long way away. That meant that sometime before morning we'd have a thundershower. Which meant that Mr. Sikes wouldn't have to get out the water truck and sprinkle the riding ring to dampen down the dust, and Mom wouldn't have to water the lawn.

"If it rains," Tamara said idly, "Mr. Sikes won't have to sprinkle the ring."

"And Mom won't have to water the lawn," I said in the same easy way.

"I wouldn't want to live where there aren't any fireflies," Tamara said. "You know."

"Yeah, I know what you mean," I said.

We sat for a while, then, watching the fireflies and the occasional lightning. It was one of those moments when everything seems perfect and you want it to go on forever. Yet, when you try to think about why it's so perfect, you can't put your finger on it, because there isn't anything really outstanding there for you to put your finger on. Nevertheless, you do feel good and you know that it's the kind of moment you will look back on when you are about seventy years old and say, "I remember that time."